# ZERO TRUST

## BOOKS BY JAN THOMPSON

**Binary Hackers** (4 Books)
JanThompson.com/binary

**Protector Sweethearts** (6 Books)
JanThompson.com/protector

**Defender Sweethearts** (6 Books)
JanThompson.com/defender

**Savannah Sweethearts** (11 Books)
JanThompson.com/savannah

**Vacation Sweethearts** (8 Books)
JanThompson.com/vacation

**Seaside Chapel** (6 Books)
JanThompson.com/seaside

Keep up with Jan Thompson's book news:
JanThompson.com/newsletter

# ZERO TRUST

BINARY HACKERS
BOOK 4

JAN THOMPSON

GEORGIA
PRESS

Zero Trust (Binary Hackers Book 4)

eBook ISBN: 978-1-944188-82-5
Paperback ISBN: 978-1-944188-83-2

*To my Lord and Savior, Jesus Christ, who died on
the cross to save me from my sins and rose again
from the grave to give me eternal life in heaven.*

*For God so loved the world that He gave His only
begotten Son, that whoever believes in Him should
not perish but have everlasting life.*
*—John 3:16*

# ABOUT THE BINARY HACKERS SERIES
## INSPIRATIONAL ROMANTIC TECHNOTHRILLERS

From *USA Today* bestselling author Jan Thompson come these inspirational near-future cyberthrillers combining technothriller and romance, featuring computer specialists living at the edge of cyberspace, where they have to juggle being law-abiding truth-telling Christians while carrying out their assignments by any and all means possible. If you're looking for clean futuristic romantic suspense thrillers that don't compromise the Christian faith, these books are for you.

The **Binary Hackers** series is set in the same story world as Jan's other books, and characters from the other series may make cameo appearances in this series and vice versa. Happy reading!

- Book 1: Zero Sum
- Book 2: Zero Day
- Book 3: Zero Base
- Book 4: Zero Trust

Binary Hackers
JanThompson.com/binary

# YOU ARE READING ZERO TRUST
## BINARY HACKERS BOOK 4

*An untrusting vigilante.*
*An unpredictable survivalist.*
*An untraceable killer.*

When trust-fund-baby-turned-vigilante Mira Proskouriakova hires jobless former soldier Briscoe Hall to help her assassinate her mother's killer, she doesn't expect to target her own father.

*Zero Trust* is book 4 in *USA Today* bestselling author Jan Thompson's Binary Hackers series of near-future technothriller stories with a side of inspirational romance. We first met Mira and her father as side characters in *Zero Sum* (Binary Hackers Book 1). Now Mira headlines her own story in *Zero Trust*.

A daughter's dangerous mission...

Back in *Zero Sum* (Binary Hackers Book 1), when Mirabella "Mira" Proskouriakova finds out that Dmitri Proskouriakoff is her biological father, she goes undercover as his housekeeper in the hope of learning how her mother was murdered. A home invasion reveals that Dmitri knows Mira is his daughter, but neither one does anything about their shared secret.

Fast forward to the present day, Mira's relationship with her father is still tenuous at best because Mira thinks Dmitri could have done a better job protecting her mother. To make it worse, it doesn't seem to bother him that his former lover and the mother of his child is mysteriously dead.

If Dmitri doesn't care, then it's up to Mira. She decides that her final mission in life is to find her mother's killer and execute her own vigilante justice. She is willing to go to death row for it. But first, she has to hire an assassin who can handle the weapon for her. Who would gladly take ten million dollars in pure gold?

Her father's designated protector...

A former US Army veteran with no job prospect, Briscoe Hall wanders aimlessly in life, and finds himself returning home to the survivalist community in North Georgia that took him off the streets when he was an orphaned kid and raised him all the way through college.

His adopted older brother and leader of the village knows that Briscoe wants to reset his career and then he will disappear from their lives yet again, being the wayfaring stranger that he is. He gives Briscoe an assignment that he cannot refuse. Ten million dollars in cash to keep Mira alive and ten million in gold to help her meet her goals. He can start a new life wherever he wants.

Her mother's killer is still at large...

An easy payday for Briscoe turns into a nightmare when the killer discovers their whereabouts in the wintry North Georgia Mountains. No matter what they do, the killer is right on top of them or a step ahead of them. Why is their enemy so set on killing Mira? What is Mira's real identity?

The only option left is for Briscoe to take Mira off the grid so that the killer cannot map their whereabouts. January weather is usually mild in Georgia, but this year, a rare snowstorm blankets the mountains in freezing temperature.

Hiding off-grid suddenly becomes a not-so-bright idea when the assassin tracks them down anyway. How on earth? Is digital native Mira still connected to the internet? How can survivalist Briscoe keep them both alive when he can't protect her from herself?

Zero Trust (Binary Hackers Book 4)
JanThompson.com/zerotrust

Binary Hackers
JanThompson.com/binary

Book News from Jan Thompson:
JanThompson.com/newsletter

# ZERO TRUST

# CHAPTER ONE

Compared to the bitter cold winters of some of the places he had traveled to after his discharge from the United States Army, January in the North Georgia Mountains felt like early fall to Briscoe Hall. He stepped outside the log cabin at sunrise, wearing only a long-sleeve hooded sweatshirt and a pair of sweatpants. He'd warm up soon enough.

The temperature was just a tad below freezing, the air was fresh, the dew on the grass had frozen into ice crystals, and nobody was fishing on the lake on the other side of the lawn.

He closed his eyes, breathing in the peace and quiet.

He stretched his muscles, then realized that his

shirt and pants were a bit tight for him. He hated to borrow anything from his brother, but there he was, wearing Tyrone's clothes and sleeping in his cabin.

Briscoe could've claimed that he had bartered his room and board if he'd brought a fresh kill from the forest—even a rabbit would do—but he had been late by three years arriving at the thousand-acre forested private property, and he didn't want Tyrone to wait any longer.

He'd been gone too much due to situations he'd been too ashamed to admit to Mr. Perfect Brother, such as being stuck in a foreign country with no documentation, no money, and no food. Wandering around jobless and homeless would've been easier in the United States, but not in North Africa. Six months into his poverty, he became desperate. The only people who would hire him and feed him were themselves on the run from the authorities.

In a moment of absurd mental opacity, he'd joined hundreds of mercenary soldiers testing Buchanan Industries' latest exoskeleton line that they'd been peddling on the dark web. The compensation they'd offered could've funded his cost of living for the next five years.

If he survived that long.

Yeah, what he didn't know could've killed him.

By the mercy of God, Briscoe had been one of

the fortunate ones waiting for nine months at the back of the line for surgical implants—the procedure abruptly disrupted by his trio of saviors. He'd had a chance to thank Dario and Iseul for his rescue, but not the third person, Leland, who'd given up her seat on the tram out of the bat cave.

More than a year later, he had yet to see Leland again. One of these days, he'd stop at Binary Systems in Atlanta and bring her a gift.

It had taken him that long to muster up enough humility to travel home to the Still Waters mountain community to see his brother, his only family, albeit an adopted one. Tyrone had been so happy to see him last evening that he seemed to have forgotten all the trouble Briscoe had brought upon the Hall family and the North Georgia mountain hideaway in the last three years.

But the catch.

There was always a catch, wasn't there? Tyrone hadn't picked him up at the airport alone. He had armed bodyguards with him, who then drove the brothers to an undisclosed private hangar, where—to Briscoe's surprise—an old friend greeted him, standing next to his private jet and a crate of cash.

Yes, a crate.

Dmitri Proskouriakoff had aged, and his full head of hair was all white. At seventy-five the man had a drive about him. However, he'd sold his shares of Moscow Mechanics cybernetics laboratory so that it could become a subsidiary of VenomLabs.

Did that mean Dmitri was retiring? If so, under what capacity had he intercepted Briscoe en route to Still Waters?

"The money is a non-issue," Dmitri said. "I only have one daughter, and I want her safe and sound."

"Something is not adding up." Briscoe could walk away if he wanted to. "You're paying me ten million dollars in cash to go along with your daughter's plan to pay me another ten million dollars in gold to take down an assassin?"

"I would've paid you less, but if Mira finds out, she's going to think she's not important to me."

"So you're showing that you care by matching her fee?"

"Something like that. You were a sniper, after all. A total of twenty million dollars should make you happy, right? Take the money and leave. That's what you always do."

Dmitri's words hurt, but he was right. Briscoe had always been a transient. A wayfaring stranger in his own community, he hadn't stayed for more than a few weeks at Still Waters since he'd left for the US Army at eighteen. Every time he stayed in one place, he wanted to move on.

Dmitri put his hand on the left side of his chest. "My heart can't take this. Why I retired from the Company. I don't have time to clean up my daughter's mess."

"Then call Watchfire Security to protect her," Briscoe suggested. "I'm just a down-and-out former soldier who is also retired."

"Perfect for the job. You have nothing to lose." Dmitri smiled. "Besides, Mira trusts you. She doesn't trust me—her own wonderful father. Nor does she truly trust anyone who has worked for me in the past—including Espy and, therefore, Watchfire, who is here in the shadows."

In the shadows?

Briscoe felt sorry for overworked Esperanza Diaz-Mendenhall. Back in the days when Watchfire Security had been a small outfit called Mendenhall Security, Esperanza and her now-deceased husband had confined their work to a small group of regular clients. Since the merger and expansion of her protective services, Esperanza had been running non-stop around the clock.

Tyrone put a hand on Briscoe's shoulder. "You won't be alone. We're behind you."

"We? Who are you referring to?" Briscoe asked.

"Still Waters Security is assisting."

Briscoe was surprised. "This is the first time your team is wandering outside the community."

"No, actually. You weren't here three years ago when Dmitri called us to assist."

"Rarely then." Briscoe didn't ask what had happened then. If it had concerned Briscoe, Tyrone would've told him. "Now you're helping again."

"Yeah. Mira bought a cabin in Still Waters, so technically she's one of us."

"Interesting." Briscoe wanted a briefing.

"I'll let Ty start." Dmitri set the alarm on his watch. "I have a plane to catch in two hours. People are waiting for me at a meeting in Prague."

Prague? As in Europe?

If Mira's life was in danger here in Georgia, why would Dmitri's mind be on another continent? Being fatherless, Briscoe wondered what sort of father Dmitri was to Mira.

Tyrone nodded. "For now, let's just say this. Dmitri's wonderful daughter announced on the dark web that she's looking for someone who can help her hunt for her mother's murderer."

"You can't be serious." Briscoe did not believe that Mira would do such a thing. She was a smart roboticist, right?

Then again, five years ago, Mira had moved to

Dahlonega to work undercover as a housekeeper in her father's farmhouse. Since Dmitri hadn't seen her since her pimpled days in high school, he had almost missed the resemblance between Mira and himself. Of course, he figured it out after two days, although he decided to play along with his daughter's charade, if only to keep her near him, where she'd be safe.

Briscoe shook his head at the father and daughter. Eccentric didn't begin to describe them.

Mira made a poor undercover housekeeper since she didn't cook and hated cleaning, but still, Briscoe found her intriguing. Never a dull moment, as they said.

"Sounds like a genius move on her part to tell the world about a new and future murder," Briscoe added.

"Please don't insult my genes," Dmitri snapped. "She's testing how much I care for her. She puts herself in danger, knowing that I'll come running to rescue her. Then she can say, 'So why couldn't you protect Mom?' Or whatever it is she's holding against me."

"We've already fended off all the former FSB agents who came after her." Tyrone shook his head. "You might not know this, but Watchfire has set up a perimeter outside Still Waters. Mira is safe as long as she doesn't leave our community."

"Okay, so what's the problem?" Briscoe stretched in the hangar. He nearly tripped over the crate of cash.

"Her bait is working." Tyrone's eyes were on Briscoe. "Word is, Karakurt is in Georgia. She's heading this way. Still Waters can only protect Mira for so long."

"Back up. Karakurt?"

"The assassin we suspect killed Svetlana nine years ago." Dmitri sighed. "No one knows what she looks like or where she came from, why she killed Svetlana, or what their relationship was. She's a mystery."

"No information?" It surprised Briscoe. "You have FSB connections, Dmitri."

"Yes, I do. However, Karakurt's history is a black hole. All we have is a name."

"You know her gender."

"That's what we're going with, based on a recording. It could've been a deep fake voice, for all we know."

Briscoe nodded. "That is to say, you don't know for a fact that it's a single individual."

Dmitri stared at him. "You're right."

Briscoe shrugged.

"There were rumblings two weeks ago that Karakurt heard Mira's call to action." Dmitri sighed again. "I pleaded with Mira to drop her quest, but she refused. Stubborn, like her mother."

*And father*, Briscoe didn't say.

"We investigated everyone who ever worked for Svetlana, and I kept thinking it could be one of her bodyguards, but they were all loyal, and most had served her for over ten years. She treated them all like her own siblings, especially her personal assistant, who was named in her will."

A thought occurred to Briscoe. "Why isn't Watchfire in this meeting?"

"Because they already know everything we're telling you, bro." Tyrone produced his phone and swiped it. He texted something and then put away the phone. "Your job is a bit different than theirs."

"Your one job is to go along with my daughter's plans." Dmitri's finger almost jabbed Briscoe's chest. "If she wants you to hold a weapon in the direction she points, do it."

"If she wants me to fire it?"

"Fire it."

"Why can't she do it herself?" Briscoe asked. No one responded. "I could end up in jail."

"Twenty million dollars awaits you after you get out." Dmitri laughed.

"You cannot be serious."

"Don't scare him, Old Mac," Tyrone corrected his friend. "Watchfire will take out Karakurt as soon as we figure out who that is. You just stick to Mira."

"Playing bodyguard would make us both bait."

Dmitri didn't directly respond to Briscoe's statement. "If I had a choice, Mira wouldn't be out there, drawing attention."

"You can't coddle her," Tyrone said. "If she wants to find closure for her mother's death, that's her decision."

"If she ends up dead?"

"Then she ends up dead," Tyrone said.

"No. I won't permit it." Dmitri pointed a finger at Tyrone. "Don't give me the 'we all die' spiel."

Tyrone said nothing.

"Are you asking for more than ten million?" Dmitri asked Briscoe. "Name your price. I don't care. Mira is my only daughter. I don't have other kids as far as I know."

Briscoe could see the resemblance between father and daughter even though they were forty-five years apart. Two stubborn people who had to have their way.

"If she's so important to you, then I'm the wrong person to hire." Briscoe folded his arms across his chest, wondering how much ten million dollars in hundred dollar bills would weigh. Mentally, he calculated that it had to be at least two hundred pounds.

What about all the gold that Mira had offered him—at least, that Tyrone said she was willing to part with? He wondered if ten million dollars of gold would weigh twice as much as the cash. Where would he store all those bars and bills while he was out there hunting with Mira?

"Take the money." Dmitri kicked the crate.

"Maybe I should meet with Mira before I give you an answer." Briscoe would take the job if Mira insisted, but he wanted to see her first. If there was something else between the lines, he was sure he could extract that out of Mira face to face.

After all, Mira trusted him.

"That works. She wants to meet with you tomorrow anyway." Tyrone glanced at Dmitri. "Wish Old Mac hadn't fought with Mira last week. Now she won't talk to him, and she's wary of me."

"She's like her mother. She has to learn things the hard way." Dmitri didn't apologize. "This will all be over when Karakurt shows herself."

Briscoe felt the weight of the task. Suddenly he didn't want the ten million dollars at all.

*Wait, twenty million dollars in total.*

"Maybe I'm not the right person for this job." Briscoe cleared his throat. "Let Watchfire do everything. You save ten million dollars." He'd still have the other ten million from Mira.

"No cold feet. Play along."

Tyrone seemed to agree with Dmitri. "We have your back. What's one assassin? Three years ago we took out a whole swarm of drones and saved everyone."

"Mira named you." Dmitri didn't elaborate. "I wish she'd trust me—her own flesh-and-blood father."

"You're intimidating." Tyrone pointed to Briscoe. "My brother here has a soft spot for damsels in distress."

"Mira is stronger than you think." Briscoe surprised himself by coming to her defense. "Having said that, I hardly know her. Just because we ate meals together a couple of times three years ago doesn't mean I'm her best friend now."

"You must be important to her. Otherwise, why would she pay for your rescue from Bitteria?" Tyrone flinched, as though he had disclosed a secret.

"She what?" Briscoe's jaw dropped.

Tyrone ignored him.

"None of her plans makes sense to me. I think

she's pretending to be crazy. I know she's more intelligent than that." Dmitri looked utterly frustrated. "I don't understand my own daughter."

*Neither do I.*

The conversation still played in Briscoe's head the morning after as the early light rose in the sky.

Mira had paid for his rescue from Buchanan Industries. Why? In the year since Briscoe had escaped Bitteria, no one had told him about Mira's involvement. In retrospect, he should have suspected something since Leland was their mutual friend.

Mira probably had the answers—and knew the secrets.

If anything bothered Briscoe, it would be not knowing the truth. Perhaps by working with Mira, he would unearth how he ended up working at Buchanan Industries. Perhaps it hadn't been as random as he'd thought.

He checked his analog watch and started jogging along the stone path that went around the lake.

Instinctively he went down the trail to the left of the cabin door, even though he hadn't been home in a while. He remembered the route because beyond the grove of hickory oak trees was Alicia's cabin.

She was the first person he had asked for upon his arrival the night before. Unfortunately, his favorite resident of Still Waters had died in her sleep two months short of her ninetieth birthday.

Was the cabin empty? Maybe he could buy it.

Then again, he hadn't planned to be in Still Waters long.

*Two more weeks and I'm out of here.*

A transient, Tyrone had called him.

"When are you going to settle down and help me farm the land?" Tyrone had asked numerous times in past years, as if hoping the answer would be different every time.

"No matter how many times you ask me, bro, the answer will always be no." Briscoe still remembered his own harsh words to his brother.

The night before, after Tyrone and Briscoe had left Dmitri in the hangar, they'd discussed the pure gold that Mira was willing to pay Briscoe. As far as Briscoe was concerned, Tyrone had never been the one to break the law, so the job offer must be legitimate.

Ten million dollars in gold.

Could he do what Dmitri and Mira had asked of him? Briscoe had tossed and turned half the night, wondering if the two concurrent tasks were worth his time and sanity. If something went wrong

—such as if he put the crosshair on the wrong person—he could go to death row for it.

Now, the sun rose slowly into the sky as Briscoe jogged. His stomach rumbled. He wasn't sure if he could wait until eight o'clock for breakfast.

He continued down the trail, knowing Alicia's cabin was coming up. He could see its roof lines peeking through the leafless deciduous trees.

He picked up speed.

"I miss you, Alicia. Wish you were my mother." He blinked away the memory.

Alicia had always fed him midnight snacks back when he had returned home once every few years. She'd sneak in a few hundred dollar bills so he could "survive out there in the wild," as she'd put it.

The memory made Briscoe smile.

Alicia had never judged him. Not even once. When the US Army discharged him under other-than-honorable conditions, Alicia had written to him every month in her fountain-pen cursive hand-writing, sharing Bible verses with him, telling him that she was praying for him.

Even though he had been out of the country most of the time and could not check his Atlanta post office box, nor could he reply to Alicia's letters, he'd been surprised that she had been a faithful friend, aunt, mother figure, and foster grandmother all rolled into one.

Alicia would know what to do about this new job. Maybe she would even have advised him to reject it, partly because she had been a woman of peace. She could've mediated a peace talk between father and daughter and settled their quarrel right here in her cabin.

Alicia was gone now—while he'd been holed up in Bitteria. For that reason he hadn't returned to Still Waters after his release, grieving on his own. He wouldn't have returned at all if Tyrone hadn't told him about this short-term contract he couldn't refuse.

With Alicia dead, the only person Briscoe could trust was God.

Who was enough.

More than enough.

When Briscoe had been stuck in Bitteria, neither Alicia nor Tyrone was there, but faithful God was.

Daily, Briscoe had prayed and sought God's will for his life. In the laboratory, he'd met nine US Navy SEALs who had been abducted by Buchanan Industries for cybernetics experimentations. He'd memorized all their names so that he could notify their next of kin if they didn't make it out alive.

Briscoe had asked them how they'd ended up there, but they wouldn't say. Oddly enough, they knew who he was. They told him that since he was there, their rescue was almost certain.

Another mystery for the ages.

One of them, Oliver Kim, had shared a Bible verse with him. Briscoe memorized Psalm 40:17 and recited that to every prisoner—which they were —day and night until help came.

> *But I am poor and needy;*
> *Yet the Lord thinks upon me.*
> *You are my help and my deliverer;*
> *Do not delay, O my God.*

As he recalled the verse now, he smiled. God had indeed delivered them. All nine SEALs went home, even though three were in flag-draped caskets. Someday Briscoe would look up Oliver Kim, who had said his father was the pastor of Midtown Chapel in Atlanta, where Leland went to church.

*See there? Another coincidence?*

No. Briscoe didn't believe it.

Once again, something else didn't add up.

Either the world was very small and Briscoe had met Oliver by chance, or someone had deliberately put everyone together. Could it be Dmitri?

As he continued to jog and think about the missing dots he couldn't connect, he smelled coffee before he saw the cabin. At first he thought it came from Alicia's old cabin. However, there was no light. All the doors and windows were locked. Curtains drawn.

The coffee smell came from the cabin next door to Alicia's. It had once belonged to her too. It was about the same size, but newer by ten or fifteen years. She'd built it for her only son, who'd never come home—not even for her funeral.

Someone was clearly staying in the second cabin, making coffee this early in the morning. Who could be living there? Certainly not Alicia's son.

He wondered if he should stop at all. He didn't want to invade the resident's privacy.

Unfortunately for him, the continuous whiffs of coffee drew his rumbling tummy, and he found himself knocking on the front door. Maybe he could just say hello and ask if the resident had known Alicia.

As soon as the door opened, a small yapping robot that looked like a Shiba Inu charged at him, making a beeline for his boots. Briscoe stepped back and almost grinned.

*Who's afraid of this little—*

He felt a sharp jolt of electricity around his ankle. The excruciating pain traveled up his legs, and he dropped to the floor, dead to the world.

# CHAPTER TWO

"Shiba One! Stop it!" Mirabella Prokouriakova yelled at the prototype Shiba Inu 3.0, which she'd been troubleshooting for the last forty-eight hours. "Get back here! Shiba!"

Shiba's jaws were still around Briscoe Hall's ankle, even as the man was out cold on the ground outside her front door. The rest of Shiba's entire body bounced up and down in excitement, little legs off the ground, its jaws still gripping Briscoe's ankle.

"Maybe Shiba didn't recognize him." Mira almost didn't herself. He looked rugged and mean now. Gone were the male-model good looks he'd had three years ago. Now he looked battle weary and worn out.

Was that a paunch sticking out of his belly?

Maybe Briscoe wasn't as fit as he used to be. Uh-oh. Did that mean he wasn't the right person for the job? She needed a sniper, not a sitter.

Mira felt bad for him. She was also still angry with Dad for banishing Briscoe the moment she'd expressed an interest in him—because Dad thought she could do better. Briscoe had disappeared for two years before Mira had found him in Bitteria, after spending several millions of dollars fishing for information. And then he went off touring the Far East for another year before he'd returned home to the States.

To think that Dad had put a tracker on Briscoe so that VenomLabs could use him to find the lost SEAL team that had been taken captive by Buchanan Industries. It had all been a setup to use Briscoe, as if he were a useless toy, easily discarded.

If she hadn't spent all that money funding the operation to save Briscoe's life, he'd be dead in Bitteria.

He was back now, wasn't he? Mira blinked, as if in disbelief that Briscoe was really right in front of her. She wanted to hug him, but Briscoe was out cold.

"Yap! Yap! Yap!"

Shiba didn't require his mouth to synthesize his bark because the speakers were on top of his head.

"Shiba! That's enough!" Mira raised her voice.

Ignoring her command more than once was a no-no, according to the user manual for the Shiba Inu Intelligent Version 3.0. Perhaps she shouldn't have bought it so early in the release. Online support groups had cited numerous bugs in this version. However, this version was not only programmable, but the open source code allowed her to transform the robot dog however she wanted.

In any case, it was too late. Two hundred and fifty dogs too late. Once out of their off-the-shelf boxes, she couldn't return them.

Not only that, she had recently bought all of Shiba Inu Intelligent stocks on a whim. Probably a result of suddenly having more money than she knew what to do with. Yes, she was now the proud owner of a company that nobody else would touch.

To be fair to herself, given time she could fix the Shiba One bugs. She might need to hire more programmers than the two in the Miami office who'd decided not to quit.

Mira ran back inside the cabin and returned with her laptop. There was no chair to sit on outside her front door. She sat down on the threshold and continued typing away—what she'd been doing all night.

Her myoelectric prosthetic left hand slowed her down tremendously, but she had learned to manage it, using two silicon-gloved fingers to peck at her keyboard and typing faster using her biological right hand.

Then she recompiled the software and pushed it to Shiba One.

Immediately the dog powered off, its jaws still attached to Briscoe's ankle.

"Briscoe?" Mira called his name.

No answer.

"Oh dear." Mira didn't know what else to do. The last thing she wanted to do was cardiopulmonary resuscitation.

She checked his airways. "You're still alive, Briscoe. Are you faking this?"

She jabbed his chest with her finger.

He didn't move.

"Stop playing."

No response.

Mira hovered her prosthetic hand over Briscoe, scanning his vitals. Her one good eye stared at Briscoe's face. She thought she saw his lips twitch slightly.

Prankster.

"Shiba One, do you want to nip him a second time?" Mira asked.

Shiba One had powered down and didn't respond. She hadn't meant it. She wanted to get a reaction from Briscoe.

"Briscoe, come on."

Still no response.

Maybe he was really passed out.

*Call Tyrone.*

She checked her pockets. No phone. "Where's my phone?"

She put down her laptop on the floor and ran around the house looking for her phone. The all-nighter she'd pulled made her dizzy now.

She finally found her phone on the kitchen counter, together with her voltage-insulating gloves —the left-hand glove larger than the right to accommodate her titanium hand.

Oh, she had left them there when she'd gone to the kitchen to make more coffee minutes ago, just before the knock on the door.

She called Tyrone on her phone as she returned to the front door, carrying the pair of gloves in her free hand. "Come get your brother. I'm sorry it's too much electricity. I tried to keep it down to fifty thousand volts—what? Is he dead? I don't know. I hope not. You want me to check? Call 911? What?"

Tyrone started yelling something unintelligible.

She peeled the phone away from her ear. *Even my own dad doesn't yell at me. Who does Tyrone think he is? Seriously.*

"I'm hanging up now. Talk to me when you're calm." Mira shook her head.

She pocketed the phone. She put on her gloves and started to pry Shiba's teeth from Briscoe's ankle.

Briscoe moaned.

If Shiba One had bugs, Mira might have to start over with Shiba Two, all the way to Shiba 250.

Only catch was there might not be enough time.

Karakurt had been upon her for two weeks, and she would probably find this community in less than thirty-six hours, the way things were going.

Any moment now Sinead Jones would text her. They were supposed to talk tonight, after she secured Briscoe's agreement to help her. He had to agree.

She had been cooped up in her cabin, out of the way, while she waited for Tyrone to persuade Briscoe to take the ten-million-dollar job. She had sweetened the deal by offering the payment in gold, something she knew Briscoe preferred to cryptocurrency.

All they had to do was lead Karakurt to a remote mountaintop cabin that Sinead and Mira had prepared. Briscoe could then swoop down for the kill. He had to believe he was the one doing it because credit could not go to Mira's real shadow team.

Would Briscoe find out?

She stared at the sleeping soul on her porch.

*Yes, this Briscoe Hall.*

Who was kind of useless at this point.

She almost smiled.

*No, he won't find out.*

Mira was about to finish separating Shiba's teeth from Briscoe's ankle, when she saw the burn marks on Briscoe's ankle. Out of curiosity, she pushed the tapered rib-knit cuff up to see how far the burn marks went. They went all the way up his calves.

Scars.

*This man has been tortured.*

Had it been in Bitteria?

She pulled his cuffs down when Briscoe moaned again.

He was waking up.

Mira leapt back, holding Shiba One in her arms. She watched Briscoe sit up.

"Did you get your power nap?" Mira asked.

Briscoe scooted back. "Keep that dog away from me."

"I'm sorry. He wasn't on a leash when I opened the door. I didn't know he'd rush out like that."

"Did you do CPR?"

"There was no need."

Briscoe's eyebrows rose. "Didn't I teach you CPR three years ago?"

"I'm not certified." It was all she could think of to say.

"So you left me passed out at your front door, waiting to die?" He stared at Shiba One.

"You're alive now, aren't you?" Mira held Shiba One tightly.

"Am I?" Briscoe checked his ankle.

Before Mira could say anything, a pickup appeared on the gravel road.

Mira took another step back. She was near the front door of her cabin. If she made a dash for it, she could run inside, lock all the doors, and close the windows and be safe. And pretend none of this had happened.

That she hadn't just tasered her assassin-for-hire.

Well, technically, her robot dog had done it.

*Bugs, didn't I say?*

Maybe Tyrone wouldn't scold her again, as though she were his little sister who could do no right. Tyrone used to be mad at Briscoe a lot, but lately he had been mad at her. She didn't know why. He should've shown her pity after what had happened to her two years ago. Then again, she hadn't told Tyrone everything.

Perhaps that had made Tyrone upset with her.

Wasn't he glad she was alive—minus an eye and a hand, but alive nonetheless?

Mira didn't understand the community leader. One moment he'd risk his life to rescue her from danger—like when Dad's farmhouse exploded three years ago—and the next moment he'd be picking on her again.

Slowly she backed away into her house between the doorframe.

"Mira!" Tyrone yelled from his cab.

Mira could hear his booming voice even before the truck engine cut off. The vehicle door slammed something fierce, making her jump.

Her mind felt fuzzy, like she needed sleep.

Yeah, she owed her body two nights of sleep.

Those software bugs had kept her up two

nights in a row, making her subsist on strong black coffee.

She had to get the bugs fixed. Shiba One and Two were critical in her mission to find and eliminate her mother's killers.

*No, I'm not going to take them to the people's court.*

Their court was waiting for them on top of the mountains.

"Mira!" Tyrone was on the porch.

He was wearing jeans stained with white paint, and his gunpowder-green barn jacket had spilled coffee on it.

She hoped that the spill hadn't been because she'd startled him by her phone call.

Briscoe was sitting up on the floorboards between Mira and Tyrone.

"Are you okay?" Tyrone placed a hand on Briscoe's shoulder.

Briscoe barely nodded.

Tyrone drew a deep breath and turned his attention to Mira. "I told you the community rules. You can't discharge firearms and stuff like that inside the property line unless we're in mortal danger."

"Technically, a Taser is not a firearm," Mira said. "It's totally legal in the state of Georgia."

"Mirabella Svetlana Proskouriakova!"

Mira's jaw dropped. Svetlana was her mother's name. Hearing it so loudly this early in the morning was too much for her.

Her lips quivered. She remembered her mother well. A beautiful socialite, half-British and half-Russian, who had somehow fallen in love with a Russian-born CIA spy. After they'd married, she could have kept her maiden name, but she decided to go the traditional Russian route and changed her last name to the feminine form of her husband's family name.

Svetlana Proskouriakova.

Dead at fifty-nine. Body never found.

Did that mean she might not really be dead? Or maybe the murderer had made it impossible for Mira to get closure.

With Tyrone's help, Briscoe rose to his feet.

"You all right, bud?" Tyrone asked.

"Yeah. I've been tasered before. I'll be fine." Briscoe stepped toward Mira, then turned around to face Tyrone.

All Mira saw was his broad shoulders in the too-tight gray sweatshirt and sweatpants. The set looked borrowed.

Briscoe was a tall man, maybe six feet two.

Mira was six inches shorter than him. She dipped her head a bit to hide behind him.

"Let's talk later. Okay, bro?" Briscoe's voice was calm. "It's probably an accident. You know Mira..."

"I don't care if she's Dmitri's daughter." Tyrone stayed rooted where he stood, but Mira could sense the tension in his voice.

"I meant that you know her methods are experimental. You remember the last time she tested the robot arm in the kitchen—"

"That was different. This time you were tasered. I guess it did a number on your brain and you're defending your assailant. That's the kind of 'experimental' you were referring to?"

Mira peeked from around Briscoe. "Bots, Ty. Bots. I only work with bots, not people."

Briscoe nodded. "You laughed when she tried to improve the robot that flips hamburgers and pancakes. Made a huge mess. Didn't hurt anyone then."

"This time we're talking fifty thousand volts of electricity," Tyrone reminded him. "For a woman who is thirty-one years old, you'd think she'd stop playing with fire."

"Correction. I'm thirty, remember?" Mira raised a hand. "Also, did you mean to say *lightning* instead of *fire*? You know, electricity and all?"

Tyrone growled.

Briscoe's arm was out, as if to prevent Tyrone from getting to her.

"Let me get this straight," Tyrone said. "She tasered you, and you're protecting her."

"You called her childish." Briscoe's arm was still out.

"I did not."

"You mentioned her age and said she still plays with fire. Don't we all? I'm thirty-two, and I'm still looking for a job."

"I offered you a job last night."

"Ah yes, almost forgot about them. The two-week project."

*Them? Plural?*

Did Briscoe misspeak, or did he really mean he had more than one job? If so, who else had hired him to work in the same two weeks? Mira had no idea at this point.

Tyrone pointed to Mira. "She said you can negotiate the fee for the job."

*Job. Singular.*

Seemed that Tyrone was trying to do damage control.

Still, Mira had heard the word disparities. She tapped her prosthetic hand, silently entering commands on the virtual keyboard to ask the computer to do some inquiries for her. She had been testing the Gauntlet prosthetic hand for VenomLabs, a cybernetics company in Atlanta that used software created by her friend Leland of Binary Systems.

"Is that right?" Briscoe turned around.

Mira quickly put her hand down by her side.

"Aren't you supposed to be a dirt-poor house-keeper who quit her job last week?" Briscoe asked.

"I guess Ty told you I stopped working at my dad's farmhouse."

"Now you're jobless too. Might you want to reconsider not paying me so much? I'm a rusty sniper, and I really don't want to use my old skills to kill people. I'd rather let the authorities do it."

"All right. I'll post a new wanted ad and hire a real assassin." Mira stepped back.

"These trust-fund babies." Tyrone laughed nervously.

Mira saw through the act. Tyrone was trying to defuse the situation.

"You know my opinion on the lack of trans-parency," Mira said. "So let me be the one to clear the air. As soon as I turned twenty-five, I had access to half of my trust fund. When I turned twenty-eight, I had full access to it. My mother left me her entire estate. She had no debt, no creditors. I can do whatever I want with it, and I'm putting it to good use looking for her murderer."

"And to find me in Bitteria." Briscoe's voice was soft.

His eyes were on hers, and that made Mira look away. To begin with, her right eye tried to x-ray his eyes, record his voice, and whatever else she hadn't told her VenomLabs proprietary prosthetic eye—with its Eagle Eye software—not to do.

"Thank you." Briscoe drew a deep breath. "If you can connect me to Leland, I'd like to thank her in person too."

"Leland?"

"Leland Yang-Joule." Briscoe nodded. "She gave up her seat for me and ended up trapped in Bitteria longer than she needed to be."

"She's home now. I'll let her know that you're eternally grateful."

"I am more grateful to you for not letting me die out there, and most grateful to God. How did you find me?"

"It wasn't easy. My dad...uh..." Mira decided against blaming Dad in front of Briscoe and Tyrone. Tyrone would only tell Dad about it. "Anyway, I'm glad you're home. I wanted to see you last night, but you'd just flown home from wherever, and I didn't want you to be surprised at the offer."

"So you asked Ty to speak to me."

"To give you time to think about it." Mira hadn't been sure how Briscoe would take it. "You might have said no."

"I haven't said yes."

"Oh."

"I have an age-old question for you." Briscoe faced Mira. "Will vengeance bring your mother back?"

"Justice will be served." If Mira could do it herself, she would, but ever since she'd lost an eye, she hadn't been able to aim as accurately as before.

Now she wanted her shooting instructor to do the deed for her.

As crazy as it was, Briscoe looked like he would say yes to ten million dollars in gold.

How long could Mira put up the charade? She didn't want Briscoe to think she was out of her mind to set an assassin to kill an assassin, although he probably did.

Having been in Christmas plays for three years in a row helped her in the amateur acting department. However, she wasn't sure how long she could keep up the charade. She was running out of scripts for an eccentric billionaire millennial.

When would Sinead call her again? Sinead was the secret sauce to this entire endeavor. Her mother's personal assistant for twenty years had promised Mira that Briscoe didn't have to pull the trigger. Sinead would take care of that, having received authorization from the British government to execute Karakurt.

Then again, did Sinead really work for the British government? Her Russian was flawless to begin with, and she had contacts in the Russian government.

All Mira and Briscoe had to do was lure Karakurt to the cabin Sinead had helped Mira to prepare in the North Georgia Mountains.

After Sinead had done the deed, she would leave the country and go home to the United Kingdom, where she hoped to raise chickens in the Cotswolds and adopt a child. Mira's mother had left her enough money to live the rest of her life without having to work again.

But first, Karakurt.

As long as Karakurt was still alive, there would be no peace for Mira.

"Why this eccentric persona?" Briscoe asked. "You weren't like this three years ago."

"I want to know who killed my mother."

"Sometimes there's fog and we can never know."

"Sometimes the fog clears. It could take a while,

but it clears." It would take time and could potentially deplete her savings.

"If you have more money than you know what to do with, I know of millions of people living in poverty and hunger every day." Briscoe kept talking.

Mira bristled. "Well, then feel free to take the gold I pay you and go help the poor."

"I might do just that."

*If we come out of this alive.*

# CHAPTER THREE

That was how Briscoe ended up in Mira's kitchen, cooking scrambled eggs for his sleepy-eyed eccentric would-be employer instead of eating breakfast with the rest of the Still Waters residents in the pavilion on the other side of the lake.

"I have many questions." Briscoe plated the eggs as the toaster popped out halved slices of blueberry bagels.

"Everyone has questions." Mira opened the silverware drawer and retrieved two sets of forks and butter knives.

"To begin with, why me?" Briscoe put the two plates on the island, in front of two barstools.

Mira walked around the island to the refrigerator. She looked for something in it.

Briscoe waited. Gave her time to think.

Finally, Mira turned around, placed a butter dish, with a half stick of butter on it, on the island.

"Which plate is mine?" she asked.

"Whichever you want."

"Coffee for you?" Mira retrieved two new cups from the cupboard.

"Thank you."

Mira poured coffee for them. Then she sat down at a barstool.

Briscoe handed her a half bagel. "Do you want a whole bagel?"

"No, this is enough. I'm cutting back on carbs."

"As you're running into the arms of assassins." Probably a bad joke, but knowing Mira, she wouldn't care.

"Are you telling me that I made a mistake hiring you because, first of all, you're not an assassin —although we could say that all US Army soldiers, especially snipers, are trained to kill, given the need?"

"With ten million dollars, you could've hired a real assassin."

"Who could very well turn on me."

"You find the right one."

"And you know someone?"

Briscoe gave her a look. "Unfortunately, I don't. I don't think Ty does either."

"I know it's very risky, but why did you say yes?"

"Hold on. I haven't agreed to help you." Briscoe hated hiding things from someone who looked vulnerable and so trusting of him. However, he had to do this because of his promise he had made to Mira's father to keep her safe.

More details of the previous evening's conversation with Dmitri came to light in Briscoe's head. He felt he had to mull over the entire conversation before he fully caught everything Dmitri and Tyrone had tried to tell him.

There was that brief second when Dmitri had said he wanted to get Mira's head examined but she refused to see a psychiatrist. He offered no explanation as to why he hadn't just come clean with his daughter about her mother's murder. All he'd said to Briscoe was that socialite Svetlana Proskouriakova had not worked for the FSB.

Apparently it had been something that Mira didn't believe to this day. Tyrone had told him on the drive to Still Waters that she believed some really outlandish conspiracy theories that should've gotten her into trouble.

Mira had insisted that she was telling the truth about her mother being an FSB agent silenced for keeping a list of the names of high-level Russian generals plotting to overthrow the Russian government and reinstating a new dynasty.

Or something silly like that.

Briscoe had a hard time believing the story because Mira had a master's degree in robotics. Why would someone as intelligent as she was come up with some unsubstantiated idea like that? This Mira, now buttering a bagel.

"Sorry that I don't have cream cheese to go with these bagels," Mira said.

"Jam?"

"None. I haven't gone to the grocery store."

"You don't have to cook," Briscoe reminded her. "Three meals are provided daily by the community kitchen."

"I know, but they eat at odd hours."

"You work at odd hours."

"I'm out of time."

Briscoe waited. *Yes, tell me more.*

"I had planned to get my Shibas activated last week, but the parts were late, and I worked alone."

Briscoe sat down.

Mira passed him the butter dish.

"Shall we say grace?" Briscoe asked.

"Oh yes, of course. I eat around the clock, and I can't remember how many times I've thanked God for keeping me alive..."

"What?" Briscoe wondered if she had misspoken. "Is your life in danger?"

Mira's right hand was shaking now. She put down her bagel on the plate, and then her left hand reached for her right hand to hold it.

"I shouldn't have done this. I made a mistake, and now I can't roll back the clock." She bowed her head. "Say grace, Briscoe."

*Wait. What did she say? What mistake?*

Briscoe wondered what it would take to keep up with this woman emotionally. What was on her mind now? What had she gone through while Briscoe had been away from Still Waters?

"Pray, Briscoe. Our eggs are getting cold," she snapped.

Briscoe cleared his throat. "God in heaven, we thank You for this breakfast. Bless us and protect us, and give us wisdom today. In the name of Jesus, I pray. Amen."

"Amen." Mira dug in to her eggs. "Told you it was cold."

"Let me reheat it in the microwave for you." Briscoe reached for her plate.

"No need. I'm going to eat it." Mira smiled at him. "Thank you for cooking these. I'm trying to learn to boil water."

"That's a good start."

"Did you learn a lot of recipes from Alicia?" Mira asked.

Briscoe nodded. "When I first came to Still Waters at thirteen, Alicia taught me everything from cooking to laundering to treating wounds to doing basic surgery."

"I don't know if basic surgery is a life skill."

"It is when you're stuck in North Africa without money or documentation and no access to medical care."

"Alicia is sorely missed. This community had relied on her nursing skills for decades."

A memory came to Briscoe's mind. "Alicia wanted to teach me to crochet, but I drew a line. I asked her to teach me to skin a rabbit instead."

"If Alicia were here, then she'd protect me." Mira drank some coffee.

"May I be frank with you?" Briscoe asked.

"Always. The moment you're not transparent, I'll fire you."

She sounded serious.

Remembering what Dmitri had told him, Briscoe had to earn Mira's trust.

"You don't have to act all crazy-like. That only makes Ty angry," Briscoe said. "He might kick you out of Still Waters."

"He won't." Mira finished eating the eggs on her plate.

"Why not?"

"Because I bought the parcels of land all around Still Waters. I will give them all to him as his reward if he helps me. That's forty thousand more acres to add to his measly thousand."

"You can't buy off everyone." Briscoe ate the last bite of bagel. He was still hungry, but these were the last bagels in the refrigerator.

"You're here, aren't you?" Mira pointed a fork at him.

"I got home late last night, and Ty was trying to explain to me what you want me to do. I haven't signed the contract."

"Plus NDA."

That too. Why would she ask him to sign a nondisclosure agreement?

"Why did you ask for me?" Briscoe picked up his plate and Mira's.

"You won't help me?" Her voice sounded broken.

Briscoe rinsed off the plates and put them into the dishwasher. This was the same dishwasher that Alicia had installed years prior.

Mira picked up her ceramic mug, but it slipped out of her prosthetic fingers, bounced off the island, and shattered on the wood floor, spilling coffee everywhere, including on Mira's slippers and jeans.

"Stand back." Briscoe held Mira's shoulders and moved her out of the way. "Tell me where the broom and dustpan are, and I will clean it up."

Mira expelled a breath. "I'm sorry. Butter fingers."

"Accidents happen." Briscoe waited for Mira to get the broom from her broom closet.

She found a rag and proceeded to rinse it under the faucet. She wrung it. "You sweep, and I'll clean up the coffee."

"Leave the rag on the counter. Go change." He swept up the broken pieces of ceramic and threw them in the trash can.

Then he wiped the coffee off the cabin floor, barstool legs, and the island. He looked around. Everything seemed clean now.

Mira returned. She looked like she had been crying, but she had washed her face.

This same woman who had plotted to take down an assassin.

Briscoe prayed that Tyrone, Dmitri, Watchfire Security, and Still Waters Security had a contingency plan should everything hit the ceiling in the next two weeks.

"You all right?" he asked.

"I knew I should've improved my shooting skills. Then I wouldn't need you. Truth be told, I'd rather solve problems through diplomatic means. I want to find my mother's killers, but you know me. I prefer to be non-confrontational."

"I'm here now. I will help you." Briscoe put away the broom and dustpan.

"You will?" Mira's eye brightened—

Only one eye brightened. Did she...

She handed Briscoe the iPad before he could say another word. "Sign here."

Briscoe read the contract. It seemed fair. He didn't bother to read it a second time. As he wrote his electronic signature with his index finger, he wondered about hidden clauses and gotcha.

Too late now.

Mira took the iPad from him with her right hand. Her prosthetic left hand was by her side.

"When did you lose your hand?" Briscoe had to know.

"Two years ago." Mira hesitated.

"I'm your friend. Tell me."

"I was following a lead. It was from the same source who told me why my mother was killed."

"How did you know about this source?"

"I hacked into Dad's computers."

"Ah, you're a hacker too?"

"Not a good one. I get by. I learned a few things from Leland. But I put my robotics skills to work. Dad's reliance on drones was his downfall."

"Were you non-confrontational when you lost your hand?"

"It was a few months before we found you. I was tracking Karakurt in Damascus. She was supposed to be hiding there, but it turned out to be a trap. Karakurt was nowhere to be found." Mira flinched. "They were coming at me at the market. I ran as fast as I could. When I turned to see if I'd escaped them, I saw a woman with her face mostly covered throw a green apple at me. I ducked too late before the 'apple' exploded. Surgeries couldn't save my eye and hand."

She stopped there.

Briscoe dared not look at her face to find scars. He had scars of his own, and they were nobody else's business. "A green apple. Does the story get juicier?"

He wondered if that came out wrong.

"Granny Smith, no less." Mira looked away, beyond the kitchen island and the small living room to the windows lining the front of the cabin.

"The type of apple is important, I see." Briscoe rinsed out a dishcloth and wiped down the electric stove top.

"Why are you mocking me?"

His attempt at adding a note of levity to an otherwise harrowing recollection had failed.

"I'm not." Briscoe stepped toward Mira, wondering if he should offer his shoulder for her to cry on. Then again, they were alone in the cabin, and thoughts of he-said-she-said popped into his head.

If he so much as touched her, he knew that Dmitri could have him killed. The former spy didn't mess around.

Briscoe walked back to the island. "Look, I'm on your side."

Even as he said it, he wasn't sure. When Dmitri matched Mira's payments, Briscoe had accepted it, so whose side was he really on? Just minutes ago he had signed the contract with Mira, knowing full well he didn't plan on killing anyone unless he had to protect Mira or save his own life.

Mira wanted him to help her assassinate her

mother's killers. Dmitri wanted him to protect Mira from her plans.

Could he do both?

Ten million dollars in gold and ten million dollars in cash said he could. However, he had to be very careful. He opened his mouth to speak.

Mira waited, cross-eyed. She blinked a few times, and her eyes looked normal again.

*What on earth?*

"Why are you blinking at me?" Briscoe asked. "Are you taking pictures with your eyes?"

"I'm not a cyborg."

"Did I say you are?" Sensing an impasse, Briscoe tried to break it. "Maybe you should give me some background information so that I'm not guessing what's going on."

"I need more coffee." Mira lifted up her mug.

"How much coffee have you had?"

"Since last night?"

"Oh. You didn't sleep at all?"

"I haven't slept since... What day is it today?"

"Wednesday."

"Oh no! I'm out of time. I have to get my Shibas debugged." Mira hopped off her barstool. "Speaking of which..."

She walked to a closed door on one side of the living room. As soon as she opened the door, an avalanche of yapping Shiba Inus escaped into the living room.

"Whoa!" With one leap, Briscoe sat on top of the island, retracting his ankles from the edge, praying the island could bear his weight. "How many do you have there?"

"Two hundred and fifty, not including Shiba One." Mira looked amused that Briscoe was sitting on the island.

"That few? Whew. I guess I needn't have worried."

"They won't bite." Mira walked toward the kitchen, with the dogs in tow. "Only Shiba One has a Taser. The rest are still in test mode."

"I see. How much did you spend on them?"

"What is the price of a human life?"

"Mine, you mean?" Briscoe stayed on the island as swarms of Shiba Inus trotted on the kitchen floor, yapping. "Can you shut them up, please?"

Mira swiped her phone and tapped here and there. The dogs stopped yapping. "There, I muted them."

"Where's the head honcho?" Briscoe asked.

"Who?"

"Shiba Whatever who tasered me?"

"Oh. Shiba One. It's deactivated right now."

"Thank you." Briscoe sat cross-legged on the island. "I feel like a stupid kid sitting here."

"We're all late bloomers."

"That's not what I mean. I want to get down to the floor and get on with my day, but you said they are all in 'test mode.' Does that mean they're dangerous?"

"Well, I bought ten of them at first, back when they were only Version 2.0, but then I needed more and more. However, they all have bugs, including the current release, Version 3.0." Mira sighed. "I've already talked to the two programmers. They're sending me patch kits. Kits, I tell you. Did they think I was joking around?"

The mention of kits reminded Briscoe of one special tracker kit that Dmitri had given him the night before as his parting gift. He hadn't had time to read the user manual.

"I need to deploy these dogs tomorrow." Mira said it in such a way that Briscoe thought she had meant to mumble it to herself.

"Why tomorrow?" Briscoe figured timing must mean something to Mira. Why the urgency?

Mira didn't reply.

"You need programmers who can handle autonomous machines such as these," Briscoe suggested. "Such as people who have previous experience with drones."

"I need debuggers. I hate debugging."

"Either way I don't know if they can fix the problem overnight, but it's worth asking."

Mira looked at him funny. "Wait. You said 'they.' Does that mean you do have people in mind?"

"Yes. They're in Still Waters. I'm surprised you haven't already thought of them."

"I haven't lived here long, remember? I only know three people from when I visited in the past: Alicia, Tyrone, you. I don't talk to anyone else, and they don't talk to me. I moved here last week because..."

"Because you had a fight with your dad and you quit your job?" Oops. That was a dead giveaway. "Ty told me."

"Did he?" Mira looked at him suspiciously. "Your brother doesn't like me, does he?"

"Maybe you need more friends."

"What?"

"Didn't Alicia try to make introductions?" Briscoe felt guilty for not being more welcoming of Mira, but three years ago he'd had problems of his own.

"She tried, but I don't have time to socialize." Mira picked up the iPad from the kitchen.

She tapped quickly with both hands, and the robot dogs trotted back into the room from whence they'd come.

Mira closed the door. "Take me to the programmers."

"Yes, ma'am." And he came down from the island.

# CHAPTER FOUR

The ten-minute walk to Havilah's barn could have been shortened if they had taken a golf cart, but Briscoe thought Mira could use some fresh air. She looked like she hadn't seen daylight in days, cooped up in her cabin all by herself.

She was dressed in a thick and warm goose down knee-length coat. Her hiking boots looked liked they could withstand a winter hike.

On the other hand, he himself was still wearing what he'd worn this morning. The air was still nippy, and he wished he'd thrown on a goose down vest on top of his hooded sweatshirt and sweatpants. So much for acting tough and all that. In reality, this was not fall.

Maybe the walk will wear her down, and she'd calm down from her crazy perch and act normal. Then again, perhaps being surrounded by two hundred and fifty Shiba Inu robot dogs was normal to Mira.

*To each her own.*

In any case, he himself needed the walk. He had barely jogged ten minutes this morning.

Along the path, neither Mira nor Brisco said nothing to each other. Briscoe supposed they were busy with their own thoughts.

Briscoe did not offer to carry either Shiba One or Shiba Two.

*Mira has arms. Let her carry forty pounds.*

Well, Mira had chosen to leave Shiba Two behind in her cabin, halving the weight she had to carry on her own. On her shoulders hung a back-pack. Briscoe didn't ask what was inside.

In a clearing, the Still Salvage barn was conspicuously quiet, with its red door shut.

"The alarm is probably on." Briscoe stopped short of knocking on the door. There was no door-bell to ring. "Let me text Havilah."

Seconds later, a side door opened. A woman rushed out, ran to Briscoe, and leapt into his arms—startling Mira, who nearly dropped Shiba One.

"My crush!" She almost kissed Briscoe.

"Havilah, please." Briscoe pried her legs off his hips.

He felt it was important to let Mira know that he was still single. He wasn't sure why, but that was his primary concern at this time.

"Shiba One could...ah..." Mira started to say.

"No no no no." Briscoe's eyes widened. "Havilah, get off me! Right now!"

"Or else what?" Havilah smiled sweetly.

"Or else her dog will Taser you."

Havilah broke free from Briscoe. "What?"

Mira stroked Shiba One's head gently.

Briscoe's eyes met hers. He shook his head quickly. "She's only twenty. Has a long life ahead of her."

"What is going on?" Havilah put her fists on her waist.

"Do you trust her?" Mira asked.

"Yes." Briscoe didn't hesitate to answer. "Maybe not with my life, but with anything related to robots and electronics. Leland trusts her."

"Then maybe we can do business—as long as she stays off you."

Now Briscoe understood more about what happened the last three years. Did Mira have a thing for him? If she hadn't, would he have been spared the one year's nightmare in Bitteria?

"Havilah, have you met Mira Proskouriakova?" Briscoe asked.

"No." Havilah cleaned her palm on her jeans, but Mira didn't shake her hands.

"She's a germaphobe," Briscoe said. "Like her father."

Havilah's eyes widened. "You're Old Mac's daughter. Can you get me a tour of his farmhouse?"

"We're not on speaking terms at the moment," Mira said. "I'm here on business. I can pay you to debug some Shiba Inus for me."

Havilah pointed to Shiba One. "That's 3.0."

"You know."

"Hottest bots. I wanted to buy one, but they're all sold out. Black market price is beyond me." Havilah nodded.

"She has two hundred and fifty of them." Briscoe turned to Mira. "If you're nice to Miss Mira, maybe she might sell you one."

"I can give you one free of charge if you can debug them all."

"Okay." Havilah extended her hand again.

Mira wouldn't shake it. "Let's sign a contract. How much do you charge per hour?"

"Fifty an hour, but we can deduct the price of one bot."

"No need if you can debug them in twenty four hours."

"Twenty four hours?" Havilah almost yelled. "I was thinking twenty four days."

"I'm out of time," Mira explained. "If I'd known about you last week, we could have five days. As it is, I can't give you more than twenty four hours."

"We have another project right now..."

"I'll double your rate if you do my project first."

"Well..."

"Triple the rate."

"Okay. I'll ask Asher if we can do it. He's our chief programmer."

"I've already debugged part of the OS. All you have to do is finish what I started. I debugged five last week, and you can use them as your template. Once you fix those five, you can replicate the process and fix the remainder. The acceleration speed is about $n \log n$."

"Roughly?"

"There is life and death involved, so the faster you fix my problems, the fewer lives will be killed."

"Wow." Havilah turned to Briscoe. "We've never dealt with life and death before. We're still studying the drones that attacked Cayson and Stella in the forest a few years ago."

"You're slow then."

Havilah gave Mira the look. She did that when she was angry and flabbergasted at the same time.

"Why are you in a hurry?" Briscoe asked Mira.

Then he remembered what Dmitri and Tyrone had talked about the day before. Karakurt was in Georgia. she was probably closing in.

Instinctively, Briscoe looked above their heads. "I think we need to go inside."

"Why? Fresh air is good for you, Briscoe," Havilah said.

"We can talk inside." Briscoe held Mira's free arm and ushered her through the door into the barn.

As soon as they entered the space, Mira's eyes widened, and Briscoe knew she was impressed.

All around them were workstations with multiple monitors. At least two dozen twenty-some-thing people busied themselves with scrolling screens and keyboards. The machines looked old. Nothing new and shiny in here. Briscoe knew that Havilah, Asher, and their team had cobbled together whatever they could salvage. They were poor college kids, after all.

"Welcome to Still Salvage," Havilah said. "I would introduce you to everyone, but you're about to yank them from a six-figure project and make them debug a bunch of broken dogs, so I want to spare you their angst."

"So I made new enemies. What's new?" Mira stepped toward the closest workstation. She inspected the old equipment.

"Nothing is wasted. We fix whatever we can salvage and turn them into these workstations, which we then use to salvage more computers and drones and bots." Havilah pointed to one side of the barn, where a team of people were disassembling what looked like drones. "Old Mac gave us some of his old drones. We have been disassembling, classifying, and repurposing them. We can't sell them to anyone, per our agreement with Old Mac."

Old Mac.

Briscoe wondered why people in Still Waters called Dmitri Old Mac.

"What kind of drones do you have?" Mira asked.

"Mostly domestic. But we have some dogs and spiders lately, coming from university labs. We go to various recycling centers and pick up some electronics and parts too."

"Can you fix a toaster?" Mira asked.

Everyone laughed.

"Are you testing us?" Havilah looked perturbed.

"I test everyone." Mira eyed Briscoe.

At that moment, he wondered if being Tasered was his test. He had thought it had been an accident. He glared at her, remembering the jolt of electricity in front of her cabin.

"A toaster?" Someone walked up to them.

Briscoe did not recognize the kid.

"This is Ipse Dixit," Asher said to Mira and Briscoe. "New hire here. Doesn't want to use his real name. His family just moved to Still Waters last month. His dad is our new pastor."

"How could you go incognito with a high profile dad in the community?" Briscoe asked.

"Online, I can."

"Thanks for the coffee," Ipse said to Mira.

"No problem. Any time."

Briscoe's curiosity perked. "What coffee?"

"Julio here lives near my cabin," Mira explained.

"Ipse!" He nudged Mira's arm. "Don't use my real name. Walls have ears."

"Ipse. Ipse." Mira laughed. "I brought them coffee as a welcome gift."

"Why?"

"Why what?" Mira ignored Briscoe. "I've been visiting Still Waters for four years, but never saw this machine room. I'm quite impressed."

"I was too, when I first got here." Ipse stood very close to Mira.

Briscoe didn't like it one bit. He hadn't pegged Mira as being sociable. However, she'd made a new friend.

Well, he was only hired to protect her, not to run her social life.

Someone else waved and came over. It was Asher, who had put on some pounds.

"You're home!" Asher hugged Briscoe.

*Home.*

Asher didn't say, "You're back!"

Briscoe wondered if Still Waters was really home. How come he felt like leaving again? One of the reasons he wanted to take Mira's offer was that it would enable him to leave. Twenty million dollars in the bank ensured that he didn't have to work for a while. He could travel and see places.

Maybe doing it safely this time.

Yeah. No more mercenary soldier whatnot for him this time. Being a tourist was safer.

"What brings y'all here?" Asher asked.

"Asher, this is Mira," Briscoe introduced her.

"I know. Old Mac's daughter."

"How did you know?"

"I work security when I'm not working here."

"Oh?" Briscoe was surprised. "Why?"

"Need the income. Still Salvage needs more income. Why this project for Cayson is important."

"Cayson Yang?" Mira asked.

Asher nodded.

"I know him and Leland," Mira said. "If I need to negotiate timing with them, let me know. I need my project done first before his. I told Havilah that you have twenty four hours."

"She wants to pay us triple our rate." Havilah looked at Asher.

"We need the money, but we're already in the middle of Cayson's project."

"Can you take some people off the project and put them on mine?" Mira asked.

"Hmm."

"Mira is giving you a free Shiba Inu on top of paying you triple," Briscoe reminded Havilah.

"If it's so urgent, why don't you ask Binary Systems to do it for you?" Asher asked. "Considering you seem to be able to pay them for it."

"Because they work with my dad, and I don't want him to know about my Shiba Inus."

"Oh."

Havilah nodded. "They got into a fight. Father and daughter are not talking to each other."

"I see."

Mira drew a deep breath. She handed Shiba One to Briscoe.

He didn't want to take it, but Shiba One looked like it had been powered down. Mira insisted, so Briscoe took the robot dog in his arm. Nothing happened, but he decided to be careful.

The robot dog didn't move when he held his belly. According to Mira, it was a male dog, but Briscoe could see that it was anatomically incorrect. Nonetheless, there was a square opening next to the serial number.

No one was paying any attention to Briscoe checking out the robot that Tasered him.

Mira swiped her phone. Tapped here and there. "How about new monitors for every workstation?"

"What?" Asher asked. "Does money grow on trees?"

"She has an orchard," Briscoe said. He really had no idea, but considering how much Mira was willing to dish out overnight, it seemed that her trust fund must be a big one.

Mira's phone pinged. She tapped some more. Then looked up. "Cayson said his project can wait a couple of days. He also said if you need his help in the next twenty four hours, you can ask him any time."

"Really?" Asher smiled to Havilah. "It's like learning from the master hacker."

"What do you mean *like*? You are learning from the master. Too bad you have to use old machines for now."

"At this rate you might as well buy Still Salvage."

"I'm not interested in buying it, but I will invest in it if you successfully debug my Shiba Inus."

Havilah pointed to Shiba One in Briscoe's arms. "What about that one?"

"This is the prototype." Mira took the robot back from Briscoe. "It doesn't leave my side. However, Shiba Two is his clone. It's in my cabin. Do you have a contract I can sign? We need to make it clear on paper what you're supposed to do for me."

That reminded Briscoe that he hadn't signed his contract with Mira. He watched Mira and Asher discuss the terms of their agreement. He could learn a few things about negotiating from Mira. She'd taken after her father, who had perfected the art of the deal.

How else could the same man send Briscoe to his death three years ago also somehow managed to persuade Briscoe to keep his daughter safe?

Maybe not. Briscoe could answer the question that Dmitri hadn't.

In all likelihood, Briscoe was only the decoy. Surely Dmitri had deployed an army of security personnel into the forest to keep Mira safe. However, that would risk tipping off Karakurt, who had an army of her own to track down Mira.

Why were they still safe?

Ipse raised a hand. "What about the toaster? Didn't you mention a toaster earlier?"

Mira nodded.

"Did you mean the toaster at Old Mac's farmhouse?"

"Have you seen it?"

"My dad took me there when he had dinner with Old Mac."

"When?" Mira asked almost too quickly.

"Last week."

"You saw a toaster?"

"It was broken. Old Mac threw it out in the trash."

"He threw out my Cook Bot 15.9?" Mira's voice sounded restrained, but Briscoe knew better.

"Old Mac said we could have it for free. I brought the container of trash here two days ago."

"Becase he knows I'm here. I'm going to see the Cook Bot, and he's sending me a message."

Briscoe didn't know how to handle Mira at this point. "What message?"

"That he's still angry with me. He threw out my invention."

Ipse, Havilah, and Asher stared at Mira. "Your invention?"

"Robotics is my real profession." When she said it, she wasn't looking at those three kids. She seemed to direct her confession to Briscoe, as if she had a need to tell him the truth about herself. "I can't cook."

"I know, but you can build a robot that does." Briscoe tried to be understanding, but he knew it was pointless.

The family was broken, and there was nothing he could do to fix it. If they were to ask him for advice, he'd tell them to just go their separate ways. He didn't care where Dmitri went, but he wondered where Mira would go.

"I will deal with Dad later," Mira said.

"Dad? Old Mac is your dad?" Ipse looked shocked. "The master roboticist has a daughter. Like father, like daughter."

"We're not at all alike." Tears pooled in Mira's eyes again. "Right now I have a bigger problem. Maybe you can go back to work, Ipse, while I discuss business with Havilah and Asher. Be kind to Cook Bot. Whether you can salvage it or not, I must have it back."

"All right," Havilah said.

"I build robots, but I'm not the best programmer," Mira started to say.

"I can attest to that." Briscoe pointed to Shiba One, still in Mira's arm.

"Please don't interrupt me." Mira straightened up. "I prefer to have a team of programmers to back me up, but right now, I don't. I have two hundred and fifty problems waiting for me. That's your challenge, should you decide to accept it."

"Oooh, a challenge." Asher rubbed his palms together, looking like a kid out of college.

Maybe he was a kid out of college. Or out of some cartoon.

Mira unzipped her backpack and pulled out an iPad. "I'm going to generate a standard contract I use with my vendors."

"Okay." Havilah shrugged. "You can trust us. We always deliver on our promises, even without a signed contract. We just ask that you don't pay us with goats, sheep, cows, and other farm animals. We prefer cash or crypto."

"Got it. Let's agree on what we need to agree on, and adjourn to my cabin. Bring a truck or something to carry the Shiba Inus back here."

Briscoe felt happy that he had helped. He didn't need a thank-you from Mira at all. He was simply contented to see that his suggestion to utilize Still Waters had benefited both parties. Mira's dogs might be properly debugged so they didn't hurt innocent passersby, and these kids out of college earned some income. It was a win-win.

He wondered if his agreements with Dmitri and Mira were also a win-win for all parties involved.

Somehow he had a feeling he was walking into a hall of mirrors.

Who could he trust? Mira or her father? Or neither?

Both of them were Christians, but who could Briscoe trust to always tell him the truth?

That remained to be seen.

Meanwhile, he was sliding on a mud, going deeper into a world that he might not have intended to get into in the first place. He had left Bitteria thanking God that he was still alive and had not been dissected on or turned into cyborgs like many others. After one year of decompression as he traveled through Asia incognito, he had been called home by Tyrone to do a job that could secure his cost of living for the next ten years or more.

He hadn't expected to be Tasered within

twenty four hours of his arrival home to the United States.

*Oh, that's right.*

Briscoe put a hand up. "Excuse me."

Everyone turned to look at him.

"Please wear insulation—head to toe, if possible," Briscoe warned. "There is danger in her cabin."

Havilah laughed. "What do you mean?"

"Full discloser, Mira," Briscoe said. "How many times have you been Tasered by Shiba Whatshisname?"

"What?" Asher's eyes widened.

"None." Mira's voice sounded upset. Maybe she didn't like to hear Briscoe bringing up the accident this morning.

"Why not?" Briscoe didn't believe her.

"Because I'm the owner. Factory setting. Any other question?"

"Clever, those product manufacturers."

"Liability and all that." Mira pointed to her iPad. "I've spelled it all out in my standard robotics contract. You can't blame me for accidentally deaths due to the Shiba Inus or anything else from my machine room, office, and cabin."

"Oooh, another challenge." Asher grinned. "Staying alive is a good goal."

Havilah rolled her eyes at Asher's remark.

"Don't we all want to stay alive?" Briscoe asked.

Mira didn't answer.

That bothered Briscoe.

A lot.

# CHAPTER FIVE

S imply on Briscoe's recommendation, Mira had hired the computer programmers from Still Salvage LLC on the spot to help her debug her Shiba Inu robot dogs. She prayed that she wouldn't regret it later.

As she led the two lead programmers, Havilah and Asher, together with Briscoe, on the path back to her cabin, Mira thought about moving the Shiba Inu Intelligent headquarters from Atlanta to Still Waters.

A new text message popped up on Mira's glass eye, projecting a screen about two feet in front of her. Her breath was frosty in the thirty-two-degree morning. She wondered when it would warm up.

She could barely see the projected virtual screen. The message was encrypted.

"I have to make a phone call," Mira said.

Briscoe stopped walking.

"No, no. You three go ahead." Mira dropped her cabin keys into his palm. "This will take just a minute. Show Havilah and Asher my home office, where the Shiba Inus are."

She turned to Havilah. "I messed up the codes pretty badly, so you might as well re-download the control software from their website. I'll give you a developer access as soon as I finish talking on the phone."

They all nodded and kept walking, except for Briscoe.

"We need to stay together," he said.

"I'm going to stand outside." Mira shivered in her goose-down coat that only went down to her knees. Her calves felt cold inside her insulated hiking pants, but her feet were warm in the wool socks and heavy hiking boots.

"Where I can see you." Briscoe eyed her hand. "Your hand looks cold. Do you have a glove?"

"I left it inside."

"Tell me where, and I'll get it for you."

"No need. I'll make this call quick and then go inside, all right?" Mira thought of her Shiba Inus.

"Show them the room and then come out if you must, but I don't want them wandering around my cabin on their own."

Briscoe nodded and disappeared into the cabin.

Mira made the call.

"Run, Mira. Run!" The voice was unmistakably Sinead's.

Yet it could've been a deep fake AI voice.

Still, could she ignore a warning like that?

She texted Sinead's private number.

MIRA

Did you warn me?

SINEAD

Why are you still standing there?

MIRA

Is Still Waters in danger?

SINEAD

Affirmative.

MIRA

There are many people here. I cannot leave.

SINEAD

You must. The Wolves are on their way.

MIRA

Who?

Addled by a lack of sleep, Mira's brain could not process what Sinead had just told her on their secure messaging app.

How did Sinead know she was still standing there? That statement alone caused Mira to doubt Sinead.

Who on earth were the Wolves? Why hadn't Sinead mentioned them before?

Would Tyrone know?

She called him. "Ty, something is going on. I just received a message telling me to run. Should I run? Or would it be a trap if I do?"

"Stay put," Tyrone barked into the phone. "I'm on my way. Where's Briscoe?"

"He's..." Mira spun around—and was startled that he was standing right there. "He's right here."

"Let me talk to him."

Mira put Tyrone on speakerphone.

"Briscoe, take Mira to the bunker under Alicia's house. Stay there until the coast is clear. Don't come out unless it's me or Old Mac."

Old Mac. Dad.

Of course Tyrone had contacted Dad. Duh. They were fast friends, after all.

"Watchfire?" Briscoe asked.

"They've been compromised."

That was a surprise to Mira. She was sure that

Esperanza Diaz-Mendenhall would get to the bottom of it. After all, Watchfire Security was her baby all the way to the days when it had been called Mendenhall Security—years before it merged with Solomon Security.

"Now, Briscoe!" Tyrone yelled into the phone as sirens blared all over Still Waters.

Havilah and Asher ran out of Mira's cabin, each carrying two Shiba Inus.

"Take cover!" they yelled as the sky darkened.

"This way!" Briscoe grabbed Mira's free hand— which turned out to be her prosthetic hand—and ran toward Alicia's cabin next door. Havilah and Asher followed.

Mira held Shiba One tightly under her right arm. There was no time to put it into her backpack.

The Gauntlet sensors in her prosthetic hand told her that Briscoe was squeezing it tightly. In front of her glass eye, data displayed, showing Briscoe's heart rate going up and his hand temperature cold.

The grove between the two cabins made it harder for them to run because of a non-existent path, plus they had to run over rocks and twigs. Mira was glad she had worn her all-terrain hiking boots, which wrapped around her ankles to protect them. Otherwise she was bound to get an ankle sprain.

Mira turned her head after she heard the swarm coming their way.

With the exception of pine trees with their evergreen needles, the rest of the trees had shed their leaves. There was no snow on the ground, but the weather was still chilly at nine in the morning. This was January, after all.

The grove ended, and Alicia's side yard began.

Briscoe led them to a trapdoor next to Alicia's bicycle shed. Mira wondered if her electric tricycle was still inside, but this was no time to check.

Briscoe had a hard time opening the trapdoor. It was not only locked, but somehow the edges had sealed shut due to misuse. He looked for tools, but there was nothing for them to use.

"Let me try." Mira handed Shiba One to Briscoe. She held the handle with her prosthetic hand and pulled with all her might.

The handle broke.

She balled her titanium hand into a fist, and was about to pound the stainless-steel trapdoor, when the drones arrived, hovering above them.

At least a dozen drones with reflective surfaces —that blended them into the blue sky peppered with morning clouds—hovered over them. The small drones looked like they had come off the shelf. In other words, they were commercial and not custom.

Whose shelf had they come from? Which company? Foreign or domestic?

"Ty, hurry up!" Briscoe pulled Mira behind him. Mira took Shiba One back.

"Anyone have weapons I can use?" Briscoe shielded Mira as they walked backward into the grove of trees. "Havilah? Anyone?"

"I don't carry any," Havilah said.

"I taught you to shoot."

"Yeah, but Dad forbade me from carrying."

"Asher?" Briscoe asked.

"I'm a pacifist—but we could throw these dogs at them. I was a shot-putter—"

Havilah slapped Asher's arms. "This is not a game, dude."

"They haven't fired at us," Briscoe said.

"They're scanning us." Mira lifted her prosthetic arm to respond in kind. "They're unarmed. They're looking for something—see their camera moving?"

Helicopter blades thwacked-thwacked above the trees, shaking the branches below them.

"Take cover!" Briscoe put his arm over Mira as all four of them squatted down.

Armed people inside the chopper fired at the drones, which dropped to the ground. Mira wanted to know who owned those drones.

More drones flew across the open field toward Mira, Briscoe, Havilah, and Asher.

Overwhelmed by the noise from the helicopter blades and exploding drones, Mira didn't hear the trucks coming, but she saw two of them park on the gravel road in front of Alicia's house. Tyrone and his people jumped out, weapons in their hands. They took up position and fired into the air.

More drones dropped.

Another truck pulled up. People whom Mira didn't recognize exited the truck. Two women dressed in black aimed their bows and arrows at the drones. One held a Japanese bow and the other a compound bow.

Mira wanted to know who they worked for. Later, perhaps—if they made it out alive. She guessed that they probably worked for Esperanza if they were on the side of Still Waters.

So busy was Mira watching the fireworks in the sky that she let her guard down for a second, hardly aware of the remaining surroundings. By the time she realized it wasn't Briscoe who'd grabbed her shoulders and lifted her three feet off the ground, it was too late.

The hexagonal formation of seven small drones connected into one super-drone reminded her of Buchanan Industries, which had been shut down the year before. She had read the report that Dmitri received after CIA protective agent Dario de la Cruz returned from Bitteria. Dmitri had shared the report with her because of his own drone brigade at the farmhouse.

The report included a historical account of the super-drone's deployment in Switzerland three years ago, when another formation of drones tried to get one Arkyn Buchanan to safety. It ended very badly for the heir to Buchanan Industries.

"Aarrgghh... Help!" The chopper and firearms were so loud that she could hardly hear herself screaming.

Briscoe's mouth opened and closed, but Mira couldn't hear him, and neither could she lip-read.

A strap appeared around her waist, tying her tightly to the drone. She screamed.

Briscoe ran and jumped, trying to catch her legs, which were outside his grasp. His face registered horror and failure at the same time.

Mira screamed, then realized it was no use.

Shiba One was still in her arms. She turned it on manually and then dropped the robot in a free fall to the ground some twenty feet below. She hoped that the robot could get help.

A corner drone broke formation, detached from the hexagon, swooped down, and caught Shiba in midair.

*No way.*

A little strap went around Shiba One's waist as the drone ascended back into its position in the super-drone, Shiba Inu hanging from it.

*Oh well.*

Mira looked down. Eagle Eye could see precisely where Briscoe, Havilah, and Asher remained on the ground. Plan B kicked in. She unlocked her prosthetic hand from her wrist and threw it at Briscoe.

Her eye captured the moment when Briscoe ran forward, leapt into the air, and caught her hand just as the super-drone lifted Mira above the trees.

"Find me, Briscoe. Track me down," Mira whispered into the wind.

*I gave him my hand.*

The super-drone picked up speed, carrying Mira away as she drew deep breaths to prevent herself from freaking out. The air was thin at this altitude, even though she could still breathe. The winter sun shone down, providing a small amount of warmth.

The wind beat her face, and she felt her cheeks freezing. Her one remaining hand pulled the insulated hood around her face, but she could use a cup of hot chocolate right now.

"At least give me a helmet!" She shivered.

She knew they had to land soon because the super-drone was big and visible from the ground. If Tyrone hadn't already tracked it via satellite, Dad would. If Dad caught up to them, it wouldn't be a pleasant day for the drone operator—or operators.

She recorded her flight away from Still Waters, across forests where she could see deer walking on the forest floor under leafless tree canopies, across mountain streams with probably icy-cold water.

The winter scape stretched up the side of a mountain range.

*Where are you taking me?*

Her eye continued to record her trip for a future court case—if it came to that.

For now, she wanted to live.

"Lord Jesus, let me live. Please don't let me get injured. I've already lost enough, don't You think?" She closed her eyes. "Please, please."

Then she realized she had to keep her eyes open to continue recording this day in her sorry life.

Whatever happened to her best-laid plans?

Now her hired assassin was back in Still Waters, away from his assignment.

Mira hadn't anticipated this knot in her two-week scheme to lure Karakurt into the forests of North Georgia, where more than one person—Briscoe not included—would take her out.

Ironically, being captured might get her closer to her target.

*Hmmm.*

The super-drone slowed as it approached what looked like a cabin at the base of a mountain slope near another stream.

Mira wondered if the stream connected to the previous streams she had seen on their flight from Still Waters. If so, Briscoe and Tyrone could track her down.

She decided it was better to save the recording now than wait until they landed. Her captors might shield her from using the internet, and none of her videos would go out.

"Find me, Briscoe," Mira said loud enough for her Eagle Eye software to record. "May God help us."

She saved the recording of her flight into an encrypted file, naming it.

"Eagle Eye, send coordinates of this place and our flight record to Briscoe Hall...and Tyrone at

Still Waters," she ordered, remembering that Briscoe had just arrived at Still Waters, so sending the file to him would be useless, as he'd have to forward it to Tyrone for processing. Tyrone was the one with the infrastructure.

Besides, Tyrone would inform Dad.

As much as she disliked him for what he'd done to Briscoe three years ago, he was still her dad, and he would come to rescue her. Maybe it would be his opportunity to make up for his past inability to save Mom.

*I must forgive him. I know...I know.*

What if she had no chance? What if today was the last time anyone saw her alive?

Her real eye turned to the sky. "Forgive me, Lord, for harboring unforgiveness in my heart. After all that You've done on the cross to save me from my own sins, I know I cannot live my life with this bitterness holed up inside me. I'm still angry with Dad, but the Bible says I need to forgive him."

Tears fell into the cold air.

The drones descended.

"I might die today, Lord. I want to make peace with Dad before I go." Her voice sped up. "In the name of Jesus, I forgive my father for not being able to save Mom. I have to accept that perhaps it was the will of God to take Mom home so young. Help me to let go of the past."

More tears fell.

Mira blinked. "Start new recording, Eagle Eye."

In a small clearing, the super-drone dismantled itself until only three drones were left, slowly lowering Mira to the ground.

Shiba One barked as his single drone dropped him off near Mira.

"Yap! Yap! Yap!"

Once the straps released, Mira and her dog reunited. She held Shiba One tightly to her chest as she looked around. The drones backed away, powering down. Mira counted eight of them, six for the six hexagon points, plus two in the middle to hold the formation together.

Where had they come from?

The front door of the cabin opened, and Mira couldn't believe her eyes.

"Sinead?" She barely voiced it.

"Mira." The forty-something woman flew from the porch, down the steps, and helped Mira to her feet.

"Thank God you arrived safely," Sinead said in her soft British accent. "I was so worried."

Mira hugged her with Shiba One in between them.

"The drones..." Mira pointed. "They look like Garuda drones."

"Yes, they are, although we wiped out their software and reprogrammed them from scratch."

Reprogrammed?

"You did?" Mira knew that Sinead hadn't told the truth. If they had erased the original Garuda software, then why did the super-drones behave in the same manner as a Garuda formation would?

*If words could show the truth, then Sinead just lied to me.*

"They were salvaged." Sinead sounded matronly whenever she wanted Mira either to stop asking more questions or to comply with her plans.

"From?" Mira asked.

"Remember when we found Briscoe a year ago in Bitteria?"

Mira nodded.

"I took the liberty of saving some drones to study."

"Without telling anyone?"

"Would I tell your dad or the FSB or CIA?"

"I don't know. How did you get them into the country though?"

Sinead didn't answer her directly.

"You saw that the drones have done something useful. They saved you." Her voice was soothing, but many questions still hung in Mira's mind.

As far as Mira knew, no one else had invaded the private property except those drones. "You said that the Wolves were attacking Still Waters."

"They were on their way before we extricated you."

"Did the Wolves arrive?"

"They aborted their mission after my drones picked you up."

"Oh." Convenient to the nth degree.

This unexpected turn of events made Mira question who Sinead really was. On the one hand, she had worked for Mom. On the other hand, had she really been loyal to Mom?

For the several months since Sinead had reappeared in her life, Mira had trusted this person more than she had her own dad. Had she been wrong to do so? If that was the case, her fallout with her dad had been needless.

Sinead stared at Mira's missing prosthetic hand. "What happened to your hand?"

"I lost it when the drones picked me up. I have two backup hands in my backpack." Mira didn't want to tell Sinead that she'd thrown Gauntlet to Briscoe on purpose. "I was so scared, Sinead."

"Shhh. Let's talk inside, where it's warm." Sinead helped her up the porch.

The cabin was larger than it looked outside. The living room stretched to the edge of the mountain, where a wraparound porch ushered in the morning sun. That meant the front of the house faced west.

"Where are we?" Mira couldn't ask Eagle Eye verbally in Sinead's presence.

"We're outside Blairsville." Sinead invited her to sit down on the plush leather sofa.

Maybe Sinead didn't think it would hurt to disclose their location to Mira. She'd find out eventually.

"Don't worry," Sinead added. "The Wolves can't find us."

The invisible Wolves.

How would Mira know Sinead was telling the truth?

"So close. No wonder the flight was short." Mira placed Shiba One on the couch. As soon as she sat down, she realized her backpack was still strapped to her back.

She set the backpack next to Shiba One. "Tell me more about the Wolves."

"Soon. Right now you need to rest. Would you like some hot cocoa?"

"You read my mind." Mira smiled. "Yes, please."

"You have your mother's smile." Sinead's voice was sweet. She sniffed a little. "Taken so young. I pray every day that you will live a long and happy life. I wish I had a daughter like you. I'd teach you everything I know."

She had always been gentle with Mira. How could this kind woman be anything but good to her? Mira remembered Sinead from her teenage years, when Mom first hired the former British MI6 operative to be her personal assistant. Sinead's years of overseas experience made her invaluable to socialite Mom.

If Mom had trusted Sinead, why would Mira doubt Sinead's loyalty now? Mira chided herself for not trusting her anymore.

At the end of the day, she knew she could only trust God. And Him alone.

"Mira?" Sinead asked.

"Sorry. I'm still stunned." Mira plopped down on the couch. "This morning has been crazy."

"Rest will help. You haven't slept in two days. Your mind is confused."

*Is it?* "I thought you were in Dahlonega somewhere. I didn't know you had a cabin in the woods."

"I was still in my hotel room in town when I

received news that Karakurt was already in Georgia. Got me scared. Had to hide, you know?"

Her voice was genuine.

Mira found her phone still in her pocket. She
swiped it. No signal.

*Huh.*

"May I make a phone call?" Mira asked.

"There are few cell towers around here."
Sinead's voice sounded genuine. "I haven't had
time to install a booster. When I do, you can make a
call."

"So you can't call out either?" Why would
Sinead be disconnected?

"Not on my personal phone, no."

See there? Sinead had evaded her question.
She had specifically mentioned her personal phone.
What about her professional phone? Work phone?
Did that work in this lodge?

Mira felt a knot in her stomach.

*Lord Jesus, please help me if I've trusted the
wrong person.*

Mira had quarreled with Dad the week before
about trust issues. She had considered her mother's
personal assistant as more trustworthy than Dad, a
former CIA spy who now worked openly with both
Moscow and Washington.

"I just thought I'd call Dad to let him know I'm

okay. He's had multiple heart attacks, and I don't want to stress him out."

"Understandable. I'll get you a working phone soon."

"Thank you." Mira put away her phone, but not before she pressed Record.

"This cabin..." Mira looked round. The furnishings were top notch. Not overly opulent, but comfortable. There was an air of masculinity. It didn't feel like it was Sinead's house. "Did you buy it furnished?"

"Yes. It was a small hunting lodge."

It looked anything but small. How much would a hunting lodge sell for these days? "How many rooms?"

"Twelve big ones. There were twenty to begin with, but they knocked down walls and merged some of the rooms to make them bigger."

"Wow." It must've taken time for her to do all that. "How much hunting land does it come with?"

"You've always been the curious one in the Proskouriakoff family."

"Am I? I ask useless questions though."

"No, they're always interesting. To answer your question, this lodge comes with three thousand acres of hunting land. Mostly deer, which need to get thinned out anyway."

Sinead spoke as though she had been in Georgia for a while.

"I'm so happy for you that you have a retreat in the woods," Mira said. "I bet the trees are beautiful in the fall."

"Very. Last fall, the leaves were especially glorious. Maybe this fall you can watch the leaves change color with me."

"I'd love to." Mira patted the couch. "I like how you've decorated this place. My dad loves these colors."

"I probably need to redecorate at some point. This was pretty much how it looked when I bought it."

"When was that?" Mira tried to keep her voice casual.

"Oh, a while back."

When was a while back?

Sinead must have forgotten she'd told Mira that she hadn't been in the United States for something like eight or nine years. Then again, couldn't one buy properties in America without setting foot here? A corporation could do it for her.

Still, Mira felt suspicious. If she went down the path of questioning Sinead, what kind of rabbit hole would she find? Among other things, her drones were problematic. Salvaged from Buchanan

Industries? That was probably a lie. After all, the CIA had first dibs. Surely they'd inventoried everything.

Besides, Sinead had never mentioned owning drones.

Or a cabin in the woods, for that matter.

But she didn't have to tell Mira everything, did she?

Mira prayed for wisdom. Until the night before, she had trusted Sinead. Now, she couldn't tell friend from foe.

She knew that God was the only one she could trust for sure. On earth, she believed she could rely on Briscoe, but he was nowhere near her right now.

*What to do, Lord?*

But first, sleep.

# CHAPTER SIX

Mira awoke with a splitting headache.
The pillow felt warm below her
matted hair. The flannel nightgown
was only barely comfortable.

She tried to remember where she was. It looked
like a guest bedroom, with the wall and ceiling
covered with pine slats. The rustic bed frame was
also wood.

"What time is it?"

Daylight streamed into the bedroom through
two windows to her left. She looked through the
clear window pane into the distance. She could see
the sky above the tree line. As the sun rose, she
lifted her palm to shield her eye.

"What happened?"

All she could remember was eating lunch with Sinead. She couldn't recall what she ate, but she'd felt sleepy after lunch. Sinead had helped her up the stairs, letting her select any of the lodge rooms she wanted to rest in. Sinead even let Mira borrow her nightgown.

The last thing she remembered was removing her prosthetic eye and hand so that they could recharge while she slept.

How could Mira have felt that sleepy? She chalked it up to the fact that she hadn't slept in two days. Shiba One's fault.

Speaking of Shiba One, where was her robot dog?

"Shiba?" Mira pulled back the blanket and climbed out of bed. "Shiba One?"

She looked everywhere in the small room, including under the bed. Shiba One was nowhere to be found. Where could he be?

She locked in her backup prosthetic hand and activated Gauntlet Two. Oh, she wished she had her original prosthetic arm, but she hoped that Briscoe was putting it to good use in geolocating her.

Sinead had carried Mira away by drones.

Why? Was that the only way to get her to safety? What about all the people at Still Waters?

Had they been safe when the Wolves arrived—
assuming the Wolves had arrived?

In the bathroom, she found a new tube of tooth-
paste and a new toothbrush. She washed her face,
brushed her teeth, and then took a shower.

Her head felt better in the hot water, but she'd
probably ask Sinead for a Tylenol.

Hands clean, she popped in her left eye and
activated Eagle Eye.

"How long did I sleep?" she asked.

*Three hours, nine minutes, twenty-one
seconds.*

"Only three hours?" No wonder she had a bad
headache. She checked her closed door. It was
unlocked. "Did anyone enter the room while I
slept?"

Eagle Eye projected the virtual screen, which
showed Mira that Sinead had entered her room
once and gently pulled Mira's blanket up to her
chin. It helped that her prosthetic eye was
autonomously omnidirectional.

Sinead didn't touch anything else in Mira's
room—not her backpack, not her prosthetics.

Which meant she probably hadn't tampered
with her things.

Still...

"Sweep, Gauntlet." Mira walked around the

small room, moving her prosthetic hand from side to side, up and down.

Nothing.

Sinead surely would have known that Mira would sweep the room for bugs, and she knew that Mira would test her. She hadn't installed listening devices in the room. She hadn't taken advantage of the situation and hacked into Gauntlet or Eagle Eye. Why not?

Perhaps Mira was wrong about Sinead. After all, Sinead had given a plausible explanation for owning drones from Buchanan Industries.

Fifteen minutes later Mira went downstairs, wearing her own clothes.

Sinead stood near the box newel post at the foot of the stairs. "You're awake. Did you sleep well?"

"I was out for only three hours, and I have a headache."

"Tylenol?"

"No, it's okay." Mira looked past Sinead to the foyer behind her. "Have you seen Shiba One?"

"No, I haven't. Isn't he in your bedroom with you?"

"I thought so, but I couldn't find him." Mira looked down the hallway and spotted Shiba One at the end of it, twenty feet away. "Shiba! Come here!"

The robot dog trotted to Mira. She picked him up. "Where have you been?"

"Interesting," Sinead said. "Did he leave your room and come downstairs?"

"Are you asking if he climbed down?" Mira smiled.

"Is he intelligent enough to take the elevator?"

"He probably tumbled down the stairs, knowing him. Factory settings, you know."

Sinead found that funny. They laughed.

A thought floated in Mira's mind. Wouldn't Sinead have cameras everywhere and would know if Shiba One fell down the stairs before asking Mira about it? She glanced at the ceiling corners, but her eye sensors did not pick up anything.

Mira's Eagle Eye software wasn't sophisticated enough to scan Sinead, who had an invisible shield around her. Mira suspected that Sinead wore implants somewhere to generate signals strong enough to scramble her scans.

Still, Mira sensed that Sinead hadn't told her everything, starting with the dubious flock of drones.

Mira didn't want to believe that she couldn't trust Sinead. Surely Sinead couldn't have been an enemy within Mira's mother's inner circle, could she?

For now, Mira had to play along. What else could she do? The signal-dampening field made this entire lodge a dead zone. If Sinead was a friend, why would she block Mira from communicating with Briscoe and Tyrone?

"You look worried," Sinead said.

"Do I? I think it's my headache making me frown."

"Maybe. I offered you Tylenol."

"I know. I might need some if my headache doesn't go away in a few hours." Mira didn't want to tell Sinead that she didn't trust her anymore after the appearance of those Garuda drones. Therefore, she wasn't about to take a tablet from her. Who knew what Sinead might put in the medicine.

"All right."

Mira's stomach growled. "Guess I'm hungry again."

*Oh dear.* What if Sinead drugged the food? Mira felt that she had to suspect everything that was unwrapped in this lodge. Earlier, she had eaten lunch without thinking.

After her power nap—which was what three hours of sleep felt like—she now realized that owning Garuda drones and then transporting them to the United States required some feat because Sinead had obviously bypassed Department of

Homeland Security checks on the importation of goods that the CIA should've confiscated in Bitteria.

In short, Sinead was in possession of contraband. How did she get the drones into the country?

"Would you like a little something? Snacks, perhaps?" Sinead asked. "You and I have to be somewhere, but we'll be back sometime this evening. We'll eat dinner out."

"Somewhere? Where?"

"I'll tell you in a minute. Do you want snacks?"

Why would she be worried about Mira being hungry if she were the enemy? Mira tried to read Sinead's face.

At the back of Mira's mind, she knew she had to contact Briscoe, Tyrone, Esperanza, Dad, and everyone else who could rescue her. If her hunch was right, she had to leave this cabin—leave the signal-dampening field—so that Gauntlet One, in Briscoe's possession, could communicate with her backup Gauntlet software. By triangulating her position, Esperanza could send a rescue team.

"Do you have chips?" *In a sealed bag, please?*

"I'll take you to the pantry, and you can choose what you want to eat." Sinead led the way to the chef's kitchen.

The walk-in pantry was large but not fully

stocked. Mira picked up a bottled water and a few protein bars that looked like they hadn't been opened.

"Would you like some hot chocolate?" Sinead asked. "Carmello can prepare a cup for you. He'll make it from scratch using organic cocoa. It's his specialty."

"Sounds like a lot of trouble. I'll just drink water."

"All right." Sinead led the way out of the kitchen and to the dining room. "While you have your snacks, I'll bring you up to date on what's happening."

"Okay." Mira sat in a chair and ate the protein bar as Sinead filled her in, sitting across the table.

"Karakurt is moving. She's taken our bait."

"Good. Been waiting for weeks for her to do so." Munch, munch—

"Wait." Mira finished chewing. "The good news is that Karakurt is here. The bad news is that I was separated from my hired assassin when your drones picked me up."

"Briscoe Hall, you mean?"

"I paid him ten million dollars in gold. The contract said I don't get a refund if I break my end of the bargain."

"He's with my people as we speak."

Mira choked on the protein bar. She drank some water to clear her air passage. "Briscoe?"

Sinead nodded. "It's all been arranged. I'm on your side, Mira."

*Are you?*

Mira wondered what Sinead had told Briscoe to make him go with her people. "Tell me you didn't pick him up with your super-drones."

"I'll let you two catch up after he takes out Karakurt." Sinead glanced at her watch. "My associates tell me that she's meeting her handler in two hours about ten miles away from here."

"Handler?" That was news to Mira.

"Right. We don't know who."

"An FSB agent?" Even as she asked, Mira wondered if she was wrong. Why would an FSB agent decide to meet Karakurt in the North Georgia Mountains? "Ten miles in which direction?"

Sinead smiled a no-answer.

Assuming Sinead had told Mira the truth, that the lodge was located outside Blairsville, Mira tried to recall her geography of the area. Every now and then, Dad had sent her on errands to various places in North Georgia. Often they were related to their farm, but sometimes, Dad let Tyrone drive Mira around to Blairsville, Young

Harris, Hiawassee, and as far as Clayton in the east.

If they were really near Blairsville, Mira knew that if they drove ten miles north, they would get close to the border of the neighboring state of North Carolina. East, and they'd see Brasstown Bald on a clear day, the highest peak in Georgia. South, and they'd be heading toward Dahlonega, where Mira had loved to shop on her days off from work at the farmhouse.

Blairsville to Dahlonega was only about an hour of driving, and Dahlonega itself was only another hour of driving to Atlanta.

Would Karakurt and her handler meet so close to the metropolis of Atlanta, where all forces would converge against them? Mira's dad would harness the collective powers of Binary Systems and VenomLabs to break all digital barriers to track down Karakurt and destroy her.

"You'll know when you get there." Sinead's reply told Mira that distrust could go both ways.

Seeing that Sinead was not forthcoming, Mira changed her question. "How do the Wolves come into play?"

"The Wolves are our shadow enemies. They have an agenda, and Karakurt is in the way."

Mira finished chewing on her protein bar.

"Karakurt and the Wolves are enemies. Wouldn't that make the Wolves our friends?"

For the first time in many months, Mira saw Sinead flinch.

She didn't know how to read body language, but Sinead seemed nervous—for a split second. "How did the Wolves get into the United States?"

"Everybody knows that you have a porous border."

"Don't look at me. I'm not in charge of this great nation." Mira sipped some water from the bottle. It tasted fine.

"In any case, the Wolves arrived in Georgia last week." Sinead looked away.

Had Dad known? Perhaps that might explain his short fuse the week before, when they'd had their father-daughter quarrel and separation.

"Their agenda has always been to overthrow the Russian government. Their leader..."

"Is probably not named Peter."

Sinead stared at her blankly. "No. His name is Vitaly Zaitsev. He was a general until he wasn't. He's on Russia's most wanted list."

*Not Uncle Vitaly.*

Only her mother's close friend. Things were clearing up for Mira. As they said, many crimes had been committed by the people closest to the victims. Would Vitaly have ordered her mother's execution?

Mira had no idea that Vitaly was the leader of the notorious Wolves. "Is he hiding in the States also?"

"That, I don't know." Sinead remained calm.

"Why didn't you tell me these things before?"

Mira caught herself. *Be careful with your words.*

"At that time, the Wolves were not in the picture." Sinead sighed. "You attracted a lot of unwanted attention on the dark web. Now the Wolves are aware of who you are."

"Who am I to them?" Besides being the daughter of Vitaly's friend.

"Nine years ago they tried to assassinate the Russian president. Your mother and I foiled their plans. Your mother was killed, and I escaped."

"Wait. I thought you told me that Karakurt killed my mother."

"Yes. Karakurt was the Wolves' top assassin."

"Wait. Now you tell me?" *What else aren't you telling me, Sinead?*

"I don't owe you anything, Mira. Did you ask your own father the same question? How many secrets does Dmitri have? More than mine by a thousandfold. Ask him why he never went after the Wolves to avenge his wife's death."

Before Mira could say anything, Sinead hopped off her chair. "We leave in ten minutes. Feel free to continue eating here. Meet me in the foyer."

Mira took Shiba One back to her room to get her backpack. She added spare battery packs, popping them in place in Shiba's belly. She hoped it would be enough for Shiba's new mission.

If she could download a few more modules, it would help, but she had no Wi-Fi or cell access to the outside world. Something clearly had put Sinead on high alert.

In the five months since Sinead had appeared in person in Georgia, she hadn't done anything that Mira would consider unusual.

Until now.

Now Mira found out that Sinead had been in Georgia longer than five months. How long had she been in the States?

If Sinead was really a friend, she would not have cut off Mira's connection. That alone told her that she could not trust Sinead.

To make it worse, Mira had paid Briscoe to bring her closure, and he was nowhere to be found.

Now Mira felt that she owed her dad an apology.

Quietly, she prayed that Briscoe would have taken her prosthetic hand to Still Salvage. If they were clever enough, they'd realize that Gauntlet could also act as a homing beacon. All three of her prosthetic hands had been programmed to find one another if they were separated.

If Briscoe took Gauntlet to Dad, it would speed up her rescue.

However, Dad was supposed to be in Prague the rest of the month, working on a secret project with Yona Epstein, a former MOSSAD agent. He might not be reachable by phone or email at all.

Mira only knew because she'd hacked into Dad's computer and had seen his secret event calendar. She might have to apologize later, but she knew her dad would forgive her.

*Blood is thicker than water.*

Ten minutes later, sitting at the back of a windowless van, Mira had no idea which direction they were going. Sinead kept her occupied by showing her video footage of Karakurt in Texas, Louisiana, Mississippi, Alabama, and then Atlanta.

The avalanche of data crossed with Mira's headache, and her eyes glazed over. Fortunately for her, the van came to a complete stop in thirty minutes.

"Welcome to North Carolina," Sinead said.

"So we went north."

"That's correct."

Officially, Sinead had now abducted Mira across state lines. "Is Briscoe here as well?"

Sinead nodded.

*Okay, make that two people abducted in Georgia and taken to North Carolina.*

Mira doubted Briscoe had gone freely.

Sinead tried to persuade Mira to leave Shiba One behind on their surveillance in the woods, but Mira refused, even though she soon discovered that there was no signal every time she stood near Sinead. And Sinead wouldn't let her hike with anyone but her.

The forty-minute hike into the woods toward what Sinead had named Cabin 109 started out warm enough, but as the elevation rose, the climb was harder, and Mira was stuck carrying Shiba One stuffed into her backpack.

Thankfully, she had worn her hiking boots back at Still Waters when she and Briscoe had walked to the barn to meet Havilah and her Still Salvage team. When the Garuda super-drones had grabbed her, she'd still had the hiking boots on. Now they protected her in the rough unpaved path of protruding roots and rocks. Where there was no path, Sinead's people hacked a way for them.

Water kept Mira hydrated, but she didn't want to drink too much due to the lack of flushing toilets in the great outdoors.

Mira prayed for wisdom to get away from Sinead. The signal dampener all around them might have prevented Mira from accessing the internet, but she could still map the path they had taken from the mountain road where they'd parked the van to their destination, Cabin 109.

Eagle Eye on her prosthetic eye, Gauntlet on her left hand, and Shiba One in her backpack all worked together in tandem to provide her a three-dimensional guide back to the road, should she choose to escape. She knew the massive calculations the trio of software was doing would drain their batteries, but she prayed that as soon as she reached safety, Briscoe or Tyrone would find her.

In the middle of the forest, Sinead's team stopped. Mira could see condensation in the air in front of their noses as they breathed. Thirty-four degrees Fahrenheit wasn't cold enough for Mira to wear a mask, but she had pulled her hood over her head to give her warmth. She had left her beanie in her cabin at Still Waters and could not find any gloves in her goose-down coat pocket.

"Is Team Nine in place?" Sinead spoke into her earpiece in a whisper.

"Yes, ma'am."

"Team Nine?" Mira asked.

"Cabin 109, Team Nine." Sinead shrugged.

Mira and Sinead, plus their bodyguard, hid in the woods, watching livestream from Sinead's people stationed all around Cabin 109. So far there had been no activity in the perimeter or inside the cabin, where they had installed cameras in every space.

Above them, clouds gathered in the late afternoon. The air felt cooler, and the breeze picked up. Around Mira, leafless branches rustled. An occasional twig fell to the dry ground. Decomposing brown leaves lay everywhere.

Something prevented Mira's eyeball from projecting her virtual screen. It might be Sinead doing something to dampen the field around herself and Mira. Still, she had ordered her trio of software to continue recording and collecting data.

Mira had to move away from Sinead to get any signal at all. Would she be safe? All Sinead had given her was a Kevlar vest that didn't feel thick at all. No helmet though. Hadn't Mira read somewhere that Karakurt specialized in head shots?

Either Sinead didn't think that Mira was in danger, or this entire activity this afternoon was an illusion.

Or perhaps Sinead thought she'd be able to protect Mira.

After all, they were the farthest away from Cabin 109. One guard stayed with them.

Suddenly, a movement on camera.

"Game on," Sinead whispered into her earpiece.

The tablet Sinead held in her hand showed two figures walking between trees on the other side of the cabin toward the house. Their heat signature showed that one person was bigger and had more girth than the other, who was lithe and moved like an acrobat.

The thinner figure stopped at the edge of the clearing, her hand up in the air as she looked around.

Mira did not recognize her, but she looked to be about Sinead's age. Forty-something.

"Oksana Spencer." Sinead gritted her teeth. "I knew it."

"Who?" Mira whispered.

"She used to work with Vitaly. She's an assassin. I think we have our real Karakurt."

The man wore a beanie on his head and a scarf around his face. Mira thought his gait was familiar —or at least he reminded her of someone.

Sinead changed cameras to get a closer view of the duo...

*Oh no.*

Dad.

Mira gasped. "That can't be..."

Sinead hushed her.

Mira's hand was on her chest. Thump thump thump.

Dad was walking alongside Karakurt.

How could Dad be Karakurt's FSB handler? Mira thought he'd only been a CIA agent all this time.

Now it made sense why he had been reluctant to help Mira find her mother's killer—because he already knew who she was.

The live feed showed Dad unlocking the cabin door. He walked inside. Just like that.

*What if that's not Dad?*

Mira wondered if he was a doppelgänger. Was this another trick by Sinead?

Why would Dad walk into a locked cabin without checking to see who was inside? Or perhaps he was familiar with this cabin.

The camera switched again, and Sinead tapped on the window on her tablet to enlarge it. "Indoor cameras seem to be working."

The woman shut the door from the inside, pulled off her jacket, walked toward Dad, and...

They kissed.

Mira flinched and closed her eyes. "I don't know if I should be seeing this."

"Your dad's been single for nine years. You have to grant him this."

"Grant? He doesn't answer to me. I just feel weird watching Dad make out with...Karakurt."

"He knew." Sinead made a face. "I'm trying to be fair to your dad. There's no way a former FSB, then a former CIA agent, would not know something is wrong, right?"

Mira shook her head. "What on earth is Dad doing?"

"You don't know many things about your dad."

"You're saying that Dad knew who Karakurt was and hid it from me for nine years." Mira thought that what Sinead said made sense. However... "How do you know for sure that's Karakurt?"

"Your dad was supposed to be in Prague this week," Sinead said. "He didn't get on the plane."

"I stopped paying attention to his schedule last week."

"When you two quarreled." Sinead tapped on other cameras.

Mira looked away. "I think I've seen enough."

"This, you haven't seen." Sinead pointed to a third person approaching the cabin.

This man was tall, looked muscular, and was dressed in black from head to toe. The ski mask prevented his face from being seen.

"That's your Briscoe." Sinead fiddled with her earpiece. "Let him do what he told me he'd do."

"Which is?" Mira asked.

"He's going to enter the cabin and kill Karakurt."

Mira gasped again.

"What? Changed your mind? Too late, Mira. You've already paid him ten million dollars in gold. He's already signed the contract. A job is a job is a job."

"But my dad is inside!" Mira tried to pray, but she wasn't sure how to pray. She took a deep breath.

*Father God, please keep my dad safe. We fought last week, but he's still my dad, according to the DNA test results. Also, Briscoe... Please keep him safe as well. Tell him to abort the mission!*

"Our target is Karakurt," Sinead assured her. "I've already told Briscoe not to harm your dad."

"But Briscoe works for me. Shouldn't he get his instructions from me?" Mira tried to calm down.

Her chest felt tight. "It's my money he's keeping. My money, my call."

*Thou shalt not kill.*

Those four words from the Bible came to Mira's mind, unearthed through years of Sunday school and church attendance, an integral part of her life with her mother.

Why now? Perhaps it was because she had just prayed to God for her dad and Briscoe. She knew that she could not ask God for a blessing when she was behaving like a beast—looking to kill.

Christians should be peacemakers, right?

"Uh... Maybe we can just track Karakurt for now," Mira said slowly. "See who she's working for."

"She's working for your dad. Your dad is the puppet master."

"Do you have any proof?"

"I know your mother, and I know your father. Trust me on this one."

Trust.

That had been an issue for Mira today.

"Look, Mira. It's too late to call off the assignment. Just live with it."

"Live with the guilt for the rest of my life?" Mira looked up.

"You'll get over it."

"Karakurt is an assassin. Briscoe... Oh, Briscoe! He could get hurt."

"Ten million dollars says he can find a good doctor." Sinead turned her attention back to her screen.

Mira closed her eyes and prayed. She heard gunshots—several of them.

Then silence.

"It's over." Sinead rose. "I'm surprised your sniper friend pulled through for us."

"You changed the agreement," Mira snapped. "You said we would tell Briscoe that he's the assassin, but in reality, he was only the point man. Your people were supposed to teach Karakurt a lesson. Now she's dead—presumably. I want justice for my mother, but not if Briscoe goes to jail."

"I'm doing this for you, Mira, in memory of your mother. How can her soul rest in peace when her killer is out there?"

"Did you forget what we said four or five months ago?" Mira asked.

"We said many things."

"We said that, if possible, we would take Karakurt to court."

"I was only joking, Mira."

A joke? "Am I a joke to you?"

Sinead nearly nodded. It was at that very

moment that Mira realized she had trusted the wrong person. She prayed there would be time to correct it before it was too late.

Mira stood up, as if to stretch. "Dad's inside the cabin."

Sinead started walking toward the killing field.

Mira made it look like she was following her, but she started running...

The other way.

# CHAPTER SEVEN

B riscoe had stayed in his hiding place for over an hour. The clump of scraggly bushes provided no cover at all, but it was the best he could do, knowing the route that Mira would take from the hint on Gauntlet One—if she stuck to the plan she had outlined in Gauntlet One.

He had dug into the ground and covered himself with a new blanket that Watchfire Security was testing for VenomLabs. The blanket was essentially a giant flexible screen that reflected back its surroundings, almost like a mirror. That way, he could keep himself camouflaged.

It had been a long day. Firstly, he had woken up too early. Then, he was Tasered by Mira's dog. The meeting at Still Salvage was good, but the drone attack and the abduction of Mira was bad.

It had led to an emergency security meeting at the Still Salvage barn, with a not-surprising visit from Dmitri, who choppered in from his farmhouse outside Dahlonega. Wasn't he supposed to be in Prague?

Briscoe couldn't read the man. On the one hand he was upset that his only daughter had been taken away, but on the other hand, his mind seemed to be elsewhere.

The good news was that Mira had started the process of her own rescue. By leaving her prosthetic hand behind, she had provided a way for Dmitri to track her. Sparing no expense, Dmitri had called in the big guns. Binary Systems dropped everything and sent their top hackers to the rescue.

Actually, Dmitri called Leland Yang-Joule in front of everyone at Still Salvage, and asked her to track his daughter. Then they proceeded to talk in computer language that sounded gibberish to Briscoe.

In spite of that, Briscoe managed to learn that Mira's prosthetics were made by VenomLabs, the same cybernetics company that deconstructed Icarus implants, Garuda drones, and Dogs of War robots from Buchanan Industries.

Seeing Leland for the first time in a year, albeit not in person, Briscoe wanted to thank her again, but she was too busy hacking into Mira's hand.

While waiting, Briscoe joined Tyrone at the armory. He almost picked a Ruger sidearm, but decided to go with a Glock instead, although it was heavier. Plus several rounds of ammunition. The rest, Tyrone picked for him according to standard issue for his security team.

And just like that, Briscoe now had yet another job.

However, it was short-lived. Dmitri ordered them back to Still Salvage before Briscoe could shoot a few rounds a the indoor range next to the armory. Dmitri was thanking Leland when Briscoe and Tyrone walked into the meeting room. Tyrone closed the door behind them.

"Somewhere outside Blairsville?" Dmitri nearly laughed. "You mean somewhere in North Georgia."

"The signal ended in the forest in the general area," Leland said. "Either Mira went out of range or she's reached a dead zone or something."

"Wouldn't they prevent her from communicating with the outside world?" Briscoe asked.

"Normally, yes. But these are special hands.

The Gauntlet software and hardware can send homing beacon in the most treacherous places."

"Satellite?"

Leland nodded. "Plus other means."

She didn't want to explain, and Briscoe knew not to push the matter.

"The Gauntlet system can hack through firewalls," Tyrone whispered in Briscoe's ears.

Oh.

"If she's in the forest, they'd have to stay somewhere to hold her prisoner, unless they want to keep moving her," Leland said. "The more they move her, the easier it is for us to detect Gauntlet Two and Three."

"The easiest thing for them to do is find a cabin in the woods, secure it, and cut off her access to the internet," Briscoe suggested.

"I agree. A cabin. Or an underground bunker." Tyrone nodded. "Check all the cabins within ten or twenty miles of Blairsville."

"Only a bazillion cabins." Briscoe chuckled.

Dmitri was sitting in a task chair and tapping on his phone. His face still looked pale.

Onscreen, Leland put up her hand. "I think we have a new development. Looks like we have a castle you can storm."

She moved over slightly so that someone else

could join in. It turned out to be her cousin Cayson Yang who scooted into the camera's view in an office chair.

He waved to everyone. "We detected encrypted signals from one of the cabins."

"If it's encrypted, how do you know right away?" Briscoe asked.

Everyone ignored him but Tyrone.

"NSA," Tyrone whispered in his brother's ear.

If Leland had access to National Security Agency supercomputers, it told Briscoe that either Dmitri or Mira was a high-valued target.

Either that, or this entire Karakurt business had national security implications.

Well, for one thing, at least one foreign assassin was on American soil. Any minute now, Briscoe expected Department of Homeland Security agents to knock on their barn door.

"Looks like someone is tracking Karakurt," Leland said. "Or who they believed to be Karakurt. Right, Dmitri?"

Color washed out of Dmitri's face. "What do you mean?"

"This person whom the people in Cabin X— which looks like a lodge, it's so big—think is Karakurt is right now sitting inside Dmitri's farmhouse."

"No." Dmitri shook his head. "It cannot be."

"She arrived last night, didn't she?" Leland asked.

"She's the reason you canceled your flight to Prague." Tyrone looked at Dmitri. "What's her name?"

Dmitri was silent.

"Name?" Tyrone asked. "Or are you ashamed of her?"

"Nothing to be ashamed of. We're both single now." Dmitri sighed. "Oksana Spencer is her name. She's German by birth, but she went to Russia, where her mother had come from. Same as my wife, Svetlana. In fact, Oksana introduced Svetlana to the Wolves."

"Let me get this straight. Mira's abductors think that Oksana Spencer is Karakurt," Briscoe said.

"Unless everything is an illusion," Leland said.

"Like how?"

"Like if they're working together or if they're pretending and want to lure the fake Karakurt out."

"So we know for sure that she's fake?"

Leland nodded. "You tell him, Dmitri."

"Nothing to say." Dmitri rubbed his forehead. "Oksana and I met again in Prague, have things in common."

*What now?*

"Two former agents, one looking for work, and one creating a new position for her." Tyrone smiled. "Then again, it's not a chance meeting. Oksana had a previous fling with Old Mac when he was still married to Svetlana."

Leave it to Tyrone to announce Dmitri's past infidelity to the world.

"It was a long time ago, before Mira was born. I've already asked God to forgive me," Dmitri said. "It was brief. I haven't seen Oksana in a while—until she sent her resume to my office in Prague last year."

"How did she know you were in Prague?" Cayson asked.

"Good question." Either Dmitri no longer believed what Oksana had told her, or he hadn't bothered to investigate her origins.

"How did this Oksana lady end up becoming the fake Karakurt?" was Briscoe's question.

"She's no lady." Tyrone chuckled. "She's an assassin for hire."

"She's not an assassin. She's only a staffer who worked in the mailroom for Vitaly, leader of the Wolves." Dmitri's correction was quick.

"She told you." Tyrone didn't let up. "She could've said anything to stay with you."

Briscoe saw how distressed Dmitri was getting.

One way or another, Oksana had implicated Dmitri. Were Mira's suspicions of her father valid after all?

"So how did she get into the United States?" Briscoe asked.

Before anyone could answer, Briscoe's phone rang and someone who identified herself as "Sinead Jones, Mira's confidant" wanted to talk to him about the contract he'd signed to take down Karakurt.

*Signed. Past tense.*

It meant that this person knew he had signed the contract, though it had only been a couple of hours.

Briscoe held up a finger. There was silence in the meeting room.

"How do I know you are who you say you are?" Briscoe asked.

"You don't, but I've told you my name. If you want to verify who I am, ask Dmitri. He knows me."

Briscoe got to his point. "Where's Mira?"

"Your focus should be Karakurt. I will text you the location," Sinead said. "Don't bother replying. It's a throwaway phone."

She hung up.

"Sinead was my wife's personal assistant for many years." Dmitri started to sweat.

"Are you okay, Old Mac?" Tyrone was on the phone immediately, calling the community clinic.

Dmitri put up a hand. "I'm fine."

"Let's have our resident RN look at you a minute, okay?"

"All right." Dmitri conceded.

The nurse came quickly. She was pretty in her fifties, and charmed Dmitri enough to let her take his pulse. When she told him to go to the clinic for follow-up, he nodded profusely.

Behind him, the meeting room door opened. Esperanza Diaz-Mendenhall and her team of Watchfire Security personnel came in. She had brought several people with her whom Briscoe recognized, and several others he did not recognize.

At the center of attention was Esperanza herself, the tough widow who had been instrumental in shooting down the drones this morning. Standing on both sides of there was her Archer Quartet, whom Briscoe saw in action in Mira's yard.

Raynelle Glynn was the leader of the Archer Quartet. Briscoe first met her in Bitteria in that operation he'd like to forget. Married to the billionaire part-owner of Watchfire Security, Raynelle purposely went out of her way to prevent asking for favors. Esperanza said that Raynelle drew on her past CIA experience more than her connection to Benjamin Glynn, the treasure hunter.

Still, it was Raynelle who had brought to Esperanza the team of archers.

Never had Briscoe seen drones taken down by arrows, but it had happened before, according to Raynelle. The person responsible for training the archers was Neviah Arbet, who did not work for Watchfire Security, and did not want to be credited for anything. In her own words, she had come to Still Waters to make sure that her archery students didn't shame her in public.

They hadn't. Rulon Smith, who walked with two exoskeleton legs, could run faster and leap higher than any soldier whose legs were not paralyzed. He reminded Briscoe of some of the soldiers he had befriended in Bitteria. His entire episode there had been traumatic except for the friendships formed among his fellow prisoners.

Rulon was never far away from Dakara Dermott, his wife. Blinded in both eyes in the line of duty at the CIA, Dakara would go on to wear prosthetic eyes developed at VenomLabs which enabled her to see farther and process information in a different way than ordinary people with biological eyes. For some reason, Dmitri had taken a keen interest in this area of development at VenomLabs.

All four of them waved to Briscoe. He gave them two thumbs-up. "Good job, this morning."

They nodded.

"Leland texted me." Esperanza directed the statement at Dmitri. "Something important like this, and it took Leland to get me here. We were at the armory—two doors down. Easy walk here. Why did you exclude me?"

Dmitri didn't reply.

"As usual, Watchfire is here to help," Esperanza added. "The price is your trust."

"It's costly to clean up someone's mess." Tyrone's snide remark was unnecessary.

After Leland filled her in on the new information about the fake Karakurt and the phone call from Sinead Jones, Esperanza sprung into action with her Plan B, which involved leading Sinead to a cabin they could contain.

Briscoe found it interesting that everyone believed Sinead had been tracking a fake Karakurt. He wanted to ask Leland to verify that. What if the fake Karakurt was the real one? Then it would seem than Dmitri had been sleeping with the enemy.

Esperanza told them that she would find

someone in her team to disguise as Dmitri and let that person accompany the fake Karakurt to Cabin 109, where they were supposed to rendezvous in front of the mystery group who had taken Mira.

If it was really Sinead, then they knew all about her from Dmitri—although his data were nine years old because Sinead stopped working for Mira's mother after the latter passed away.

If it were the Wolves, then there was a problem. According to Esperanza, the Wolves were former generals and military people who'd tried to overthrow the Russian government and failed. Some of them had been executed, but the core group fled Russia.

And showed up in the United States?

"If Sinead and the Wolves are connected, then they aren't coming for Mira," Esperanza said. "They're after Dmitri."

Next thing Briscoe knew, had two hours to pack and leave for the border of Georgia and North Carolina. His first stop was the community storehouse to gather overnight camping gear. He hadn't camped out recently—except for those harrowing months in the deserts of Libya three years ago. However, he'd hiked and camped enough in the past to know what he needed.

North Georgia was nothing like the winter

colds of Peru or Nepal or Bitteria, but he had to be prepared in any case. He started with two negative-twenty sleeping bags, two insulated sleeping pads, and waterproof two-person popup tent. It was all he could stuff into the backpack along with freeze-dried food, a water purified, a shovel, flashlights, a small stove, firestarter, battery packs, his Bible, a change of clothes, an axe so that he could cut down small trees to build a primitive shelter, if needed, and some other essentials for winter camping.

He might have overpacked because he was nervous about hanging out with Mira. If anything happened to her, he would be under the watch of one very angry former FSB and CIA agent. Dmitri might have retired from his glory days, but he could still kill with his bare hands.

*According to Tyrone.*

Or maybe his brother was just trying to scare him.

In any case, seventy five pounds of gear later, Briscoe stopped stuffing his backpack from the Still Waters storehouse. A few residents stopped by to tell him they were praying for the mission to "rescue the eccentric princess." None of them laughed, so Briscoe knew it wasn't a joke.

The entire community wanted Mira to come home, even though most of them hardly knew her.

She was one of those residents who kept to themselves. But the single men of the community had interacted with her, as Briscoe found out from the well-wishers.

The one who wanted Mira home most of all was her father. Briscoe tested out his backpack by walking from the storehouse to the Still Salvage barn. Dmitri greeted him at the door. He looked weary, as though he had a hard time handling this entire Karakurt affair.

"I was supposed to retire from all this drama," Dmitri said quietly.

At the end of his career, Dmitri had no choice but hand his daughter's safety to Briscoe, whose only claim to fame in the old spy's eyes was that he was Tyrone's younger brother. If Tyrone trusted Briscoe, so would Dmitri.

"You hurt her and I kill you—after I torture you some." Dmitri pointed a shaky finger as Briscoe.

*Just some?*

Briscoe believed that Dmitri would do exactly as he said. Death in his hands would be brutal.

"I bring her home safely and we go fishing?" Briscoe knew that every now and then Dmitri would go to the Still Waters trout pond and fish with Tyrone as they discussed how to save the world.

"You got it." Dmitri's face lit up. He slapped Briscoe on the shoulder. "Until then, take her to Bunker 78. If, for some reason, you cannot reach Bunker 78, I'll send you some alternate routes. Where's your phone?"

"Why?"

"I'm going to load some proprietary apps on your phone. They won't be as sophisticated as Mira's apps on her hand or... Anyway, you'll have enough to get by."

Briscoe swiped his phone, entered his pin, and handed the phone to Dmitri.

Dmitri tapped on the phone. "Your phone is too old for my apps. Why don't you have the latest phone?"

"Why do I need the latest?"

Dmitri shook his head. "Keep up with technology, son."

Son?

Nobody had called him son since Alicia passed away.

"I'll get you a phone you can use," Dmitri said.

Little did Briscoe know that Dmitri would take him to Mira's cabin. Tyrone, the de facto "sheriff" of the community, came with the spare key that Mira herself had given him.

"Oh no." Briscoe didn't want go inside. "The

last time I was here, her dog Tasered me. I'm not going in there without her being here."

Dmitri looked him kinda funny. "Her life is in danger. You'll need a phone. I know I gave her a few and she has them in her machine room. I know because the GPS tells me they're still in her cabin. I can configure them in minutes for you. Also, I need you to bring her a change of clothes."

"Full disclosure: I did make her breakfast in her kitchen this morning, so it's not like I've never been inside."

Dmitri raised his eyebrows. "You made my breakfast with my daughter in her own house? Was she wearing her nightgown?"

What kind of a question was that?

Briscoe hadn't pegged Mira as someone who'd wear a nightgown. He thought she might be a pajama sort of woman.

"No, sir. She was fully clothed in regular work clothes or something like that. She hadn't slept in maybe two days." When Dmitri didn't say a word, Briscoe added. "Uh. After Shiba Tasered me, she felt sorry for me, I suppose. Fed me food as a peace offering."

Dmitri laughed.

His laughter echoed in Briscoe's mind hours later when he crouched in the bushes, waiting for

Gauntlet One to lead Gauntlet Two in his direction.

Briscoe chuckled at the memory of levity, but it was short-lived when heard some noise coming down the forest trail.

# CHAPTER EIGHT

B riscoe saw Shiba One first, bounding over the small hill with those short legs of his. Then Mira came running, panting and crying at the same time and dashing past his hideout in the bushes by the side of the trail. She couldn't have seen him due to the experimental VenomLabs blanket he had covered himself with.

He almost called out her name, just before he heard the unmistakable noise.

Drones.

Hounds going after Mira.

Still covered with the blanket attached to his backpack and carrying a Glock in his holster, he ran after Mira, caught up with her, grabbed her around her waist, and lunged into the nearest bushes just before muffling her scream with his gloved hand.

They landed poorly and rolled out into the open on the other side of the bushes, down a small hill, and into a ditch of rotting leaves. He pulled her close, covering both of them and their backpacks with the blanket of many colors. They stretched out side by side like two logs. If the blanket did its job, then they'd look like a pile of dead leaves lining the ditch.

"It's me, Briscoe," he whispered in Mira's ear.

They were in the dark under his blanket and could not see each other, but this was the closest they'd ever been, body to body. What would her dad say?

"Mmmmpphhh!" came her reply.

"Shhh," he whispered. "Drones overhead."

She pulled his hand off her mouth.

Briscoe could feel the strength of the metal grip in her prosthetic hand.

They remained quiet until the sound of drones became distant.

"I think we can get out now," Briscoe said.

Under the blanket, Mira kicked Briscoe and tried to punch his face. "Did you shoot my dad?"

"No!" He held her arms at bay. He refused to retaliate even though he'd been trained in close-contact Krav Maga by the Israeli forces in joint exercises back in his US Army days. All he could do was grab her arms and hope she didn't kick him where it mattered.

*Like the legs I need to hike ten miles to the safe house.*

"Dad was in Cabin 109." Mira's voice broke into quiet sobs.

"No, he wasn't." Briscoe lifted the blanket and moved away from Mira just in case she kicked him again.

"What?"

"I'll explain later. He's fine." So was the supposedly fake Karakurt.

A moment of silence passed.

Mira put her prosthetic hand on his arm. "Then who was that who looked like you?"

"Long story."

"Explain now."

"Three decoys." Briscoe kept his voice down. "If all goes well, the remainder of Espy's team members are storming the castle now. The lodge will be thoroughly swept."

"So everyone's alive? Including Karakurt?" Mira asked.

"That's not the real Karakurt." Or at least they

believed so at this point. "Sinead had been following the wrong person."

"No?"

"We had to trap Sinead to rescue you."

"Oh." She reached out to touch him. "Did I hurt you when I kicked you?"

"Yes." Not really. It would seem to Briscoe that Mira hadn't had any martial arts training. Or even know how to kick properly.

"I'm sorry. I get it now. Lookalikes." Mira sighed. "Which means Sinead has figured it out by now."

"If she hasn't been captured by Espy already."

"You mean her people surrounded Cabin 109 to take out Sinead's people at the perimeter?"

"That was the plan."

"How did Espy know Sinead's formation?"

"Gauntlet One."

Mira nodded. "That means even though I was unable to access the outside world on my backup Gauntlet Two and Eagle Eye and Shiba One, Leland was able to access my wearables. I don't know whether to feel happy or concerned about it."

"Military satellites, I think."

A dim light appeared on her prosthetic hand as Mira tapped a virtual keyboard. "I'm ordering Shiba One to keep going away from here."

"He'll get captured." Briscoe looked around, the loaded Glock in his hand. He should've brought something more because he couldn't imagine shooting down drones with the small handgun.

"That's the idea, but not without a chase."

Finally, Briscoe understood what Mira was doing. "A Trojan dog."

"Is everyone okay at Still Waters?" Mira asked.

"We're all fine. Thank God. The drone attack was a smoke screen for the second batch of drones to take you away."

"You mean the Wolves never attacked Still Waters?"

"They're still investigating that." It was all Briscoe could say at the time. "Either there's a possible connection between the drones and the Wolves since nobody else arrived besides the drones, or there's no connection at all and the attack was orchestrated by someone else."

"How are they getting to the bottom of it?"

"Espy and Leland are running the operation now."

"If Leland is involved, then that tells me everything I need to know."

"You trust her."

Mira nodded. "I'm not too sure about Espy because she works with my dad. However, she will tell him things as they are, not what he wants to hear, so I trust her more than I trust Dad."

"Ty also tells your dad what he thinks."

"Yes, he does, but I don't like your brother because he scares me."

"He's not that bad." Briscoe remembered standing between his brother and Mira this morning. "He has a soft spot for people in distress."

"Am I in distress?" Mira chuckled. "Leland doesn't think I'm in distress. She believed me and is on my side. She's been trying to get more information for me about my mother's activities that led to her death."

Speaking of Leland, Briscoe was amazed she had hacked into Gauntlet One to activate its homing beacon, seeking the other two prosthetic hands still with Mira. He wanted to tell Mira about that part, but he wasn't technical enough to explain a thing if Mira had questions.

All he knew was that if they could track the hands, they would pinpoint Mira's exact location.

*Which means...*

If the Wolves could hack into Gauntlet, they could also find Mira, thus putting her in grave danger.

"Mira, listen. I need you to go offline on all your devices."

"Right. We don't want to compromise our location."

Briscoe waited for her to turn off her devices, but he couldn't be sure she had. He had to take her word for it.

"I'm so relieved that my dad is still alive." Mira burst into tears.

"What I said earlier. He's fine." It felt both wrong and right for Briscoe to hold her in his arms. "Shhhh."

It wasn't like he didn't like the physical contact, but he remembered what Dmitri had told him before he left Still Waters, and he didn't want to cross the line.

Dmitri had paid him to protect his daughter. That was all.

And she had paid him to... Well, he'd have to give her a refund. After all, their circumstances had changed.

Then again, he felt that their relationship was still at the friendship level, even though he knew that Mira wanted to advance beyond that to...

What did she have in mind, exactly?

Suddenly Mira pulled away. Wiped her tears. How easily she seemed to switch gears. She tapped her prosthetic hand again. "We need to get out of here before Sinead finds us. She could be coming up behind the drones. Unless, of course, Espy got her."

"Right."

"Did you park a truck somewhere?"

"No. We'll be rescued as soon as we get to Bunker 78." He didn't want to scare her by telling her that Bunker 78 was ten miles away on foot.

"A real bunker or what?"

"I don't know for sure. I've never been there. All I know is that it's supposed to be twenty-eight degrees tonight, so we better get going."

"I need a place to regroup and rethink the mess I'm in."

"That we're both in." He paused. "It will take us three or four hours to hike, depending on the terrain and how many times we stop. We will be hiking in the dark partway. Are you up to it?"

"At night in this forest. Huh." Mira adjusted the backpack on her back. "Maybe it won't be so bad since I'm not alone anymore."

*Not alone?*

"Yes, we're never alone as long as we have God," Briscoe said.

The afternoon sun was setting. In the sunlight, Mira stared at the blanket as Briscoe folded and stuffed it into a pocket in his backpack.

"Tell me more about that blanket, Briscoe. Does it use nanotech?"

"I have no idea." Sometimes Briscoe thought the blanket had many tiny mirrors. Whether it used nanotechnology or not, that wasn't his problem.

"Where did you get it?"

"I'll tell you later."

"That's a minimum of four or five unanswered questions, Briscoe."

*Evasive maneuvers!* "Uh, do you want Gauntlet One?"

"Gimme." She pulled off her backup prosthetic hand, grabbed her original one from Briscoe, and popped it onto her left wrist. "Thank you."

"No problem. Good throw." Briscoe referred to her ingenious idea of leaving her prosthetic hand behind. "Did you think it could have been turned into a homing beacon?"

"When I programmed Gauntlet, I had the concept of a carrier pigeon in mind." Mira pressed a button on her wrist. "I figured that y'all would take it to Leland."

Briscoe wanted to say that her father did.

A semitransparent canopy appeared around them like a dome.

"What's this?" Briscoe asked.

"Our heat shield. It's experimental and may not work. Which way?"

Briscoe led the way. Mira stuck close to him.

The dome expanded to cover them as they stood together.

"If it works, then Sinead—or night creatures like bears and such—won't detect us," Mira said.

"Bears are in hibernation right now. Otherwise, they do have a keen sense of smell. The dome wouldn't be of any use."

"I was trying to be fair to Sinead. My point is that she might not be the only one after us. The Wolves might be too."

"So you know who the Wolves are?"

What else did Mira know?

"Enemies of our enemies." Mira blinked, and a screen appeared two feet in front of her.

Briscoe stared at the projected map of the forest.

"I wasn't able to see this earlier," Mira said. "Sinead blocked my signal and access to the internet. However, when we left the cabin, I believe I had access before I lost it again."

"Maybe we should use that sparingly. She could track us if we're online."

Mira shrugged. "I'm in a private network. I dare her to find me."

Her face was angry again.

"Did you have a fallout with her?" Briscoe checked his backpack to make sure nothing was missing from when they had rolled into the ditch. Everything was still there.

Then he swiped his phone, preloaded with apps from Dmitri and Leland before he and Tyrone had driven out. A map program appeared. "That way to Bunker 78."

"Is that the fastest route?" Mira looked in the same direction he did.

"Safest, yes. We'll be there in three or four hours regardless." He had come prepared, and his backpack carried all the essentials for winter camping, just in case they had to wait until daylight.

He was holding his phone with the map in it when it buzzed. A secure text from Tyrone that had penetrated the forest. NSA technology at work. It'd better be good news.

O*peration Doppelgänger a success.*
      *Lodge clear. Watchfire has Sinead. Taking her to FBI.*

*Old Mac recovering at home. Don't worry.*

*See you at Bunker 78.*

B riscoe read the text to Mira.

Color drained out of her face. "Why is Dad recovering at home?"

"I don't know. Let me ask." He texted Tyrone. The reply came immediately. "Stress."

"Oh. Thank God it's not another heart attack. Is anyone staying with him at the farmhouse?"

Briscoe wondered how much he could tell Mira about her dad and Oksana Spencer. Perhaps that was a family problem that they'd better resolve themselves...

"Who's taking care of Dad right now?" Mira asked again.

"His girlfriend."

"Name?"

"Oksana Spencer." He had to tell her the truth. "They had a relationship a long time ago, but they've started dating again."

Mira looked flustered. "What did you say? How long ago?"

"Maybe you should talk to your dad."

"If we don't get out of this forest alive, I'd never know because you held back a vital piece of information concerning my family."

Briscoe didn't answer her.

"Was Dad still married to my mother?"

Briscoe nodded slightly.

"Back there at the cabin, were the decoys reenacting a real relationship?" Mira asked.

Briscoe nodded. "I just found out today. Dmitri kept their secret well."

"Even I didn't know. Look, I'm not against him having a girlfriend. My mother has been dead for nine years. I just... Give me a minute to process this." Her eye flared. "Sinead thinks that Oksana is Karakurt."

"That's hard to believe. Would your dad date your mother's assassin?"

Mira actually shrugged. "Dad is an enigma to me."

Briscoe decided that he'd leave the rest of the story for later. "In any case, Ty said not to worry."

"Wait. Then I can recall Shiba One." Mira ordered Gauntlet to find Shiba One.

No answer.

"Where did he go?" Mira tried again. Tap. Tap. Tap.

Nothing.

"We can't go until I get Shiba One back."

"You've got to be kidding me." Briscoe strained his ears, hoping to hear yaps in the distance. "If we stay here, we're sitting ducks."

"But Ty just told you they arrested Sinead." She looked at him in a way that indicated she wanted to justify staying even though she knew that they could rule out Sinead as Karakurt.

"Five minutes." Briscoe couldn't believe he gave in.

"Thank you." Mira leapt up and hugged him.

"I don't know if a hug is worth my relenting." Yes, it was.

*Mira looks happy.*

They sat in the forest under the reflective blanket, waiting for a robot dog to respond to Mira's call.

"Are you sure no one else will intercept your call?" Briscoe felt behind the times because of his lack of technical knowledge.

Mira nodded. "I'm using a special frequency and a private satellite."

"Is that allowed?"

"Is what allowed?" Meaning: better not ask any more questions.

Briscoe remembered the meeting at the Still Salvage barn that morning, in which Tyrone mentioned the NSA. Maybe everything Mira was using or deploying had special privileges.

Why?

Briscoe heard yaps in the distance. Annoying yaps that drew closer.

And here came Shiba One—covered in red clay and mud and soil and whatnot—wagging its robotic tail...

And missing a leg.

"What happened to you?" Mira scooped up the robot dog, smearing mud all over her gray coat. "Yikes!"

"Can he track his missing leg?" Briscoe asked. "It's littering if we don't find it."

Mira turned Shiba One over, popped open the door on his belly, and accessed the panel underneath.

"That's not the best place to put an access panel, is it?" Briscoe asked.

Mira shrugged. "Let the factory know."

Minutes later they were on the trail with Shiba One in Mira's arms. She sighed. "I'm so glad Dad's alive. Even though we argue a lot, I don't want to see him injured or dead, you know?"

"I don't know if it helps, but your dad was the one who called Leland to help. He was very worried."

"We're family, after all." Mira shrugged.

"I'm outside looking in, and I hope you two will forgive each other for last week's quarrel and move on," Briscoe said. "The Bible talks about not letting the sun go down on your anger."

"Are you referring to that verse in Ephesians?" Mira blinked, and a screen appeared in front of her. "Eagle, look up Ephesians 4:26–27. Display." She read it aloud.

*"Be angry, and do not sin": do not let the sun go down on your wrath, nor give place to the devil.*

Oh. Briscoe got it now. It wasn't an implant in her head projecting a virtual screen. Mira had a prosthetic eye. She had mentioned Eagle Eye so casually that he had almost missed it. Now that she'd mentioned it, he wondered if it was the same software that Dakota Dermott, Esperanza's blind security specialist, had in both of her glass eyes.

Briscoe wondered how Mira saw him through her eye. Was she able to read his vitals? His raised heart rate, perhaps? He'd better stay calm, or else the report might reach Dmitri.

Briscoe didn't know why he felt it was necessary to please Dmitri. Perhaps he hadn't had a father figure in his life for so long that his respect for Dmitri had gone from calling him Old Mac to his real name.

In that regard, Mira was authentic. She always spoke her mind, told the bitter truth, and didn't hide her feelings. Sadly, he hadn't reciprocated.

As of today, he had missed her in the intervening hours they had been apart, after her abduction and before he'd found her again.

"We should thank God for saving you," Briscoe said.

"It's hard to pray when I'm angry."

"Are you angry?"

Mira nodded. "I'm still angry that Dad didn't do anything to save Mom."

"How do you know he didn't try?"

"If he did, he didn't try hard enough. To make it worse, I couldn't get a straight answer from him," Mira confessed. "In fact, I was so upset with him that I started a fight last week to get him to tell me the truth—everything he knows about my mother's death. Is that so hard to do? Just speak the truth."

"I'm sorry."

"Dad used to tell me that if you keep anger overnight, it will only create bitterness in your heart," Mira said. "Then he told me to stop looking for Mom's murderer. That made me angrier, you know?"

"Your dad used to work for you-know-where. They're masters at concealment."

"He no longer works in those places, right? Besides, he's a Christian. As a follower of Christ, doesn't he have to speak the truth? After all, Jesus

Christ Himself is 'the way, the truth, and the life,' as it was written in John 14:6."

Briscoe knew that verse by heart.

*Jesus said to him, "I am the way, the truth, and the life. No one comes to the Father except through Me."*

"You want your dad to tell you the truth behind your mom's death," Briscoe said. "But have you considered that perhaps he himself doesn't have the information you seek?"

"Why can't he find it?"

Briscoe smiled. "You put your dad on a pedestal, don't you?"

"No, I don't."

"I used to put Tyrone on a pedestal. He could do no wrong. He was near perfect. Then one day he disappointed me, and I got upset and stopped trusting people. It took me a few years to understand that God alone should be on the pedestal, and God alone is whom I really need to trust with all my heart, soul, and might."

"Dad is not God."

"Right. I hate to say that you should expect to be disappointed by your fellow sinners, but I would urge you to turn your eyes on God instead."

"I hear you but Dad made me so angry. I'd forgive him, but then he'd make me angry again."

"You let him."

"How do I let go of this anger? Sinead said that passive anger is also anger."

"Sinead, the woman who abducted you?"

"What she said is true though."

"She put your life in danger. What if the drones had dropped you from thirty feet in the air?"

"Esther 4:16 says, 'If I perish, I perish.' I go to heaven and see Mom again."

"I don't want you to die."

"Who am I to you?" Mira laughed.

Briscoe didn't want to answer her. Instead, he said, "Ask God to help you to forgive your dad again. Seventy times seven. Remember?"

"Do you have to remind me of that verse?"

"Two verses. Matthew 18:21–22." Another Bible passage that Briscoe had memorized.

*Then Peter came to Him and said, "Lord, how often shall my brother sin against me, and I forgive him? Up to seven times?" Jesus said to him, "I do not say to you, up to seven times, but up to seventy times seven."*

"Your dad has had a hard life and had multiple

heart attacks," Briscoe said. "Who knows how long he'll live."

"To a ripe old age."

"You know that we don't know that. Only God knows how long we live."

"You're right. I'm just being..."

"Mira, my point is that if you have problems with a fellow Christian, it would be hard for you to worship God with a clean heart and clear conscience—"

Briscoe stopped talking so abruptly that he startled Mira.

He swung his arm out, stopping in front of Mira's waist. "Step back."

The path ended in a T-junction, but Briscoe's only map on his phone didn't show which fork to take. His map said to go straight. "Straight" would mean over...

A cliff!

# CHAPTER NINE

At the edge of the cliff, Mira took the opportunity to unload her backpack and stretch. "Maybe there was a suspension bridge or something that was washed out by a rainstorm."

"I don't see signs of that, do you?" Briscoe looked around, anxiety etched on his face.

"Nature reclaims itself very quickly." Mira offered to help Briscoe remove his backpack. He refused her help.

"Regardless, a non-existent bridge is of no use to us." He checked his scanned map again. There was nothing on the map that indicated the type of pathway ahead.

"Let me see." Mira grabbed the phone from

Briscoe without a *please*, and pinched open with two fingers to zoom in the map. "Who drew this crude map?"

Briscoe didn't reply.

"Looks like something from your brother. He's such a troglodyte."

A small grin appeared at the edge of Briscoe's lips.

Yep, they both knew Tyrone.

"The map didn't come from Ty."

"No?"

"Then again, because he doesn't use technology as much, he's taught me to live off the grid. That's coming in handy now."

Mira's eyes were still on the map. She snapped a photo of it with her Eagle Eye software.

She tapped and dragged her index finger. "Once we get to the other side, there's more hiking to do."

She stepped to the edge of the cliff.

"Careful." Briscoe's arm went around Mira's waist.

"I just want to see what's on the other side." Mira pushed his arm away.

"Sorry. I didn't mean to..."

"Don't worry about it. If you see me about to fall off the cliff, do whatever you can to catch me."

"I will. Would you do the same for me?"

"Sure. This is how a buddy system works."

"Are we buddies?" Briscoe stood next to Mira, looking out.

"We are now." Mira handed his phone back to him.

They stood silently for at least thirty seconds while Mira stared ahead and here and there. She was glad they weren't talking as she surveyed the area.

"Eagle, scan and survey," she whispered.

She was operating a prototype Eagle Eye, and it took a lot of her to communicate with the glass eye. Eagle Eye was not a point of being able to read her mind. That would require an implant in her brain, and Mira wasn't ready.

In fact, she wanted to try it, but Dad said no. He was so vehement in his protest that it scared Mira into not trying at all. To drive in the point, Dad would always mention Cayson Yang, who nearly died when Buchanan Industries implanted Icarus into the side of his head against his will. Several others had died as a result.

Mira walked along the cliff, and Briscoe followed her. "When was the last time it rained?"

"Maybe last week? I can't remember precisely. I

checked the weather report when Ty drove me here, but only briefly."

"Between then and now, this part fell off the cliff." Mira pointed to a sheer drop-off and the red clay on it.

"Looks like it."

Mira stopped. "I think we should get our backpacks."

"Stay here and I'll bring them back." Briscoe started to move.

Mira grabbed his arm. "No. We need to stick together. I don't want to admit it but I'm a little bit scared."

Mira wanted to be transparent with Briscoe. She hoped that he would reciprocate. So far she had lost trust in so many people that there were only a few people left whom she felt she could rely on. One of them was Briscoe.

However, she hadn't seen him in three years. Had he changed? She couldn't tell until she could test his trustworthiness.

"Don't be scared. I'm here." Briscoe's voice was quiet, assuring.

"Thanks. Let's go."

Briscoe nodded. "Sunset is in half an hour. We need to get to Bunker 78 soon."

"If we don't know where to go, are we lost? Just asking for philosophical research."

Briscoe ignored the remark. "We probably have bit of daylight after sunset, and then it's dark. I have a flashlight, but navigation is going to be difficult in a forest like this."

"Even with Shiba One. However, better something than nothing, right? I can map your crude map to my digital map of the forest."

When they reached their backpacks, Mira noticed how bulky Briscoe's was. "Hey, how about distributing some weight? Let me carry something."

"I can handle seventy five pounds. Back in my Army days, I carried more than this."

"Super hero you."

"I'm not boasting."

"I can take Shiba one out of my backpack and carry him in my arms. How about I stuff a sleeping bag or something into the main compartment?"

"If you want to. Remember that you're still carrying Shiba on top of the backpack weight." Briscoe unzipped his backpack. Took out a sleeping bag and pad. They were rolled up.

"Yeah. I think I can squeeze them in. Let me move things around bit to make room."

She moved her laptop, satellite phone, batteries,

cables, backup prosthetics, spare clothes, toiletries, and whatnots into an expanded compartment.

Then she took the sleeping bag from Briscoe. "Is this mine?"

"Yeah. It goes down to negative twenty, so we should be nice and toasty in Georgia."

"Thank God we're not in Wyoming. Last winter, Dad had a meeting in Jackson Hole, and I went. It was so cold that I thought my ears were going to fall off." She pointed to her goose down coat. "That's when I bought this, but I kid you not, my mind was thinking I should have been in the Caribbean."

"That would be a nice place to go."

"Have you been?"

"A few times to St. John's and the Bahamas. I'd like to go back someday. Lately I've been traveling through Asia." Briscoe hesitated. Then added, "I only came home for this job."

"Maybe consider this as a travel job, even though you had to travel home." Mira stuffed the rolled up from mat next to the sleeping bag.

"If not for this job, I wouldn't be back in the States this soon."

*I know.*

Briscoe was holding a few packs of freeze-dried meals when Mira looked up.

"Why don't you carry those?" She asked.

"I have more. These are for you to carry, just in case we get separated. You'll need water and food."

"Good idea." Mira stuffed the meal packs in the backpack pockets. "I don't have any water."

"We'll have to share for now, When we get to a stream, I'll filter some water."

"I can't drink filtered water." Mira zipped up her backpack. "I get a stomach ache. I can only drink boiled filter water."

"We'll boil some water for you. Hot water will keep us warm."

Briscoe lifted Mira's backpack over her shoulders. "Hope that's not too heavy for you."

"It's my equipment that's heavy. The backpack and pad are bulky, but they're lighter than my battery packs."

"Right."

In no time, they were ready to get on the trail. "I need to survey the valley a bit more. Then I can give Eagle and Gauntlet time to create a new map for us."

"Better hurry before we get tracked."

Mira nodded. She ordered Eagle Eye to merge what it saw with Briscoe's map and her own map, and then feed it to Shiba One, still in "sleep mode" to run internal backups of what it saw along the trail when Sinead's drones were chasing it.

"Let's walk." Mira went ahead of Briscoe. "Would you like to hold Shiba?"

"Is he powered down?"

"No. He's sleeping."

"Does that mean he won't Taser me?"

"I told you he's a prototype. I'm still debugging it."

"Then, sorry, I cannot carry your dog for you."

"No problem." Mira was happy that Shiba One had returned to her.

"Unless he doesn't mind dangling from my backpack like a canteen."

"He's already lost a leg." Mira grinned. "I don't need him to lose more body parts."

"Considering Sinead's been arrested, we might not need to hurry as much."

"You're assuming Sinead is Karakurt." The whole idea of this operation was to find Karakurt. Now that there were news of two potential Karakurt candidates, Mira felt that someone else might be pulling invisible pupper strings.

Who? Dad? The Wolves? FSB? CIA?

"I'm not." Briscoe walked alongside Mira. "It would be great if this is over, but I wonder if we're not peeling enough layers off this problem yet."

"Something is wrong with our situation, and I can't pin it down."

"You have that feeling too?" Briscoe raised his eyebrows.

"Are you going to wiggle your eyebrows for effect?"

"Like this?" His eyebrows made waves.

Mira laughed.

"Made your day?"

"Hardly, Mr. Hall." Mira smiled. "I'm glad you're here instead of Ty. He and I don't get along too well. He thinks I'm...eccentric."

"You're unconventional. What I like."

*What he likes?*

"Are you trying to tell me something I didn't know?" Mira stopped at a tree that was clinging for dear life at the edge of the cliff, as though the soil had suddenly given way.

Briscoe cleared his throat. "I was thinking that if it snows, we might consider setting up a tent and wait it out. If it doesn't snow, we could hike at night and make it to Bunker 78 in three hours."

"Oh, I see." Mira stopped pursuing his other thought. It might have been fleeting, for all she knew. "I prefer to hike to a five-star hotel with a flushing toilet, but here we are."

"If you camp outdoors, you can see billions of stars in the sky, and not just five."

"You won't see any stars at all if you're dead."

"We don't have a choice. If the weather gets bad tonight, we have to stop and take shelter."

"How bad is the weather going to be?"

"It's slated to snow tonight, so it'll be rough."

"Snow or sleet?" It seemed adventurous to Mira. "I've never camped out in the snow before—and at night, to boot."

"As long as we don't get hypothermia, we'll last until daybreak, when we can see better where we're going."

"I defer the camping decisions to you, Briscoe. I'm a city girl. I don't do outdoors very well unless I can drive around in my car."

Her eyes spotted something about the cliffs. The "valley" looked more like crater. "Something is wrong about this valley. Doesn't it look more like a crater to you?"

The sun was setting but they could still see the other side.

The more she walked along the edge of the cliff, the more usual this phenomenon was. Rather than a valley, this looked more and more like a...

"Sinkhole," they said in unison.

Eagle Eye continued scanning.

"This sinkhole is three-quarter miles in diameter and half a mile wide deep," Mira announced.

"How did you know?"

"I eyeballed it."

"You what?"

"The point is, if we had hiked at night, we might have fallen into it. Do you think anyone would find us? Like a tree falling in the forest."

"God knows, though."

Mira pointed here and there. "Look at the unusual features. The trail there is cut off abruptly. The tree lines look unnatural. Like the earth suddenly opened up and swallowed the ground."

Briscoe nodded. "Maybe the sinkhole wasn't there when the map was drawn."

"Or someone tampered with the map on your phone, and gave you an old map without the sinkhole."

"This phone is from your cabin." Briscoe produced the phone and waved it in front of Mira.

"I don't own such a phone—wait. You entered my cabin?"

"Ty has the key. He let us in."

"You and Espy?"

"No. Me and your..."

Mira's shoulders sagged. "My dad. Just as I've

suspected. Did you see him pick up the phone from my office or did he pull it out of his magic pocket?"

"Ah... If you put it that way..."

"My dad is using us as bait to cach Karakurt."

"He wouldn't use his own daughter, would he?"

"He used his own wife to track down enemies of the FSB."

"He did?"

"Some say it was only hearsay. I wasn't born then, but that was how they met. Mom was a socialite informant."

"Sinead told you all that."

"Yes."

"Is it possible that she might not have told you the entire truth?"

"There are corroborative evidence. For example, even though you said that the Karakurt at Cabin 109 today was fake, Sinead had spent months tracking her all the way from Prague to here. Her research is thorough. I've inspected them using independent sources."

"Yet how could she be so wrong about Karakurt?"

"This is a first for her. She'd worked for my mother until the day she died, and she is a very meticulous person. No loose ends."

"I don't know what to tell you because I don't know all the facts."

"They're hidden from us." To make the truth about Karakurt known, Mira knew then and there that they had to continue being the bait. "Did you bring your sniper rifle?"

"It's at Bunker 78." Briscoe looked like he regretted not carrying it with him.

"So what's in your backpack?"

"Small little thing. Can't take out Karakurt unless I get close."

"I'd say you already failed your mission. I want a refund."

"Now you want a refund."

"Have you already spent it all?"

"Day one, Mira."

Before Mira could give him a vote of no confidence, light snow started to fall all around them. "Uh-oh."

"It's almost dark now, and we're stuck in the forest. I think we need to find shelter before dusk, or we'll be out in the cold." Briscoe looked around. "Look for somewhere we can pitch a tent."

"We could both die tonight."

"Maybe. Maybe not."

Mira searched her coat pockets for her phone.

"I'm going to call Espy to pick us up. I have a lot left to do in my life, and want to live."

"Watchfire Security has been compromised, so she's on a skeletal crew right now."

"Are you sure?" Mira was surprised that Esperanza didn't reply to her text right away.

"According to what I learned this morning while we were scrambling to find you." Briscoe hesitated.

Mira texted Esperanza again. No answer. She called her. No one picked up.

"Even if they answer, can they find us under this heat bubble we're in?"

Mira almost forgot she was walking inside a heat shield with Briscoe. "I don't know. It's beta."

"Beta as in a prototype?"

"Something like that." Mira wasn't sure how to explain the differences to a civilian.

"So, beta as in it might not even work. You just don't know, right?"

"Have you ever seen software that works perfectly?" Mira asked.

"I get your point." Briscoe laughed. "If Espy's outfit is compromised at such a time as this has has go tot be related to Karakurt. Wouldn't you say?"

"Your guess is as good as mine."

"What about Karakurt then? And your mission to seek justice for your mother's murder?"

"This whole quest is to draw her out."

"And yet we're quitting just as it gets dark and cold."

"No, we're not quitting. We're going back to our warm cabins at Still Waters, get a good night's sleep, and then go from there."

"I have to tell you that your father is a part of the rescue team."

"Of course he is. He's always in the thick of things."

"Ty told me that Espy couldn't get Leland off another project to help us. However, your dad was instrumental in calling Leland's boss. Next thing we knew, Leland she dropped everything to help us find you."

"Tell her thank you."

"I already did. She gave up her seat in the trolley to save me back in Bitteria, and I won't forget it."

"She's like that. So we know one person we can really trust." Mira texted Leland. Also no reply.

*What is going on?*

Mira closed her eyes and drew a deep breath.

When she opened her eyes, Briscoe was flicking

snow off her hair. "You might want to put your hood on."

Mira did so without a word.

She called Leland again. No response. "My phone is not working."

"Should I use my phone?" Briscoe asked.

"No. Don't use anything my dad gives you."

"Why not?"

"Because he'll own you."

His eyes widened.

"He did pay you, didn't he? I bet he matched my fee." Mira tried texting Leland and Esperanza again.

Still no response.

"Why don't you come right out and say it, Briscoe Hall? You owe me that much." Mira steeled her voice. "I don't have time to beat around the bush. I've only slept for three hours in two days, and I'm tired of people lying to me. They lie in so many ways it's not even funny anymore. Even my own dad lies to me. Don't lie to me, Briscoe."

"I'm on your side."

"Are you? Then speak the truth."

"Have I lied to you?"

"Omitting information is a form of lying."

"What do you want to know?" Briscoe's voice softened.

"If my dad hired you to do something at the same time." *I might hold it all against you, but I still deserve to be told the truth.*

And so Briscoe did. He told her about being intercepted on the way to Atlanta by Dmitri, who matched her offer of ten million dollars.

"You took my money and you took Dad's money." Mira didn't know what to say. "Either you're greedy or you think you can do both jobs well."

"They're both two sides of the same coin. Your father wants me to protect you from danger. You want me to help you track down Karakurt. As for that, Karakurt has come to us, so I hardly did anything about it."

"She comes to us so easily, as if the wants us to know who she is," Mira said.

"She. That bothers me."

"What?"

"Is Karakurt really a woman?" Briscoe asked. "How do you know the assassin is not a man?"

"We don't, but we're trying to be fair. Not all killers are men."

Briscoe nodded. "True but we literally have no idea."

"Hence her." Back in the old days, the English language defaulted to "he" when the pronoun is unknown. "To use them interchangeably would be confusing."

"I guess."

More snow fell, now mixed with sleet, making the path muddy. The mess on the ground would surely hide their shoe prints.

The temperature was dropping rapidly.

"We'll talk later. Ler's find shelter now."

"Yes, ma'am." Briscoe busied himself scoping out a site in the waning light. "I think we can stop here and pitch a tent near that rock. The trees are not close enough to worry me."

"Yeah, I'd be worried about snow-laden branches falling on us."

Briscoe pointed east, basically in the direction of the sinkhole. "If we face the morning sun—that way—we will get some warmth when we get up in the morning."

Briscoe's voice sounded grave, as if he regretted taking on this double assignment.

Mira didn't blame him.

They could both die in the forest tonight, and nobody would know.

# CHAPTER TEN

---

Briscoe was determined to get to Bunker 78 because he trusted Dmitri. Briscoe believed him when he said his girlfriend was simply Oksana, an non-combatant mailroom clerk.

After walking along the sinkhole cliff with Mira, Briscoe wondered how they were going to get to Bunker 78 without a GPS.

For now, they had to find a place to sleep overnight. When daylight came, they would be able to see their hiking trail more clearly.

Mira helped him pitch the waterproof tent on a dry patch of ground by an outcropping of granite. They lined the bottom of the tent with a reflective ground sheet that Tyrone had insisted Briscoe bring.

*Thank you, big brother.*

"This tent is awfully small," Mira said.

"It's a two-person tent. Ty and I might have used this one on the rare occasions that we camped together." Briscoe unfolded the self-inflating foam-lined sleeping pads and blew into them to inflate them.

"But you're brothers. We're not."

"We can put our backpacks between us to act like a wall."

"Okay."

Briscoe lined up the two sleeping pads side by side.

"There's hardly any room though," Mira said.

"It's just for one night. We're fully clothed. We'll be in our own mummy sleeping bags. God is our witness."

Mira nodded.

"Besides, your father knows we might camp out." In fact, the whole Still Waters community knew. "This is survival camping. We're not on a romantic interlude."

"No. Of course not."

"If it makes you feel better, we can take turns sleeping. We can toss a coin to see who gets the first watch." Briscoe arranged the mummy sleeping bags next to each other. "These can keep you warm at negative twenty degrees."

"I'll stay up first."

"Fine." Briscoe invited her into the tent. "Let's get out of the snow."

They shook off their hiking boots.

"Dinner?" Briscoe asked.

"I'm thirsty."

"We're running out of water, but I'll catch fresh snow and melt it." Briscoe looked for a pan of some sort in his backpack.

"Boil snow?"

"Yes. I remember you need boiled water to drink. Tell you what. I'll do it twice. First I'll melt the snow and then filter that before we boil it."

"Sounds good. I'm sorry I'm difficult."

Briscoe looked squarely at Mira. "You're not difficult. I find you intriguing, but don't tell your dad, or something might happen to me."

Mira chuckled. "You might disappear."

*Again.*

It didn't sound like a joke, but Dmitri was not beyond threats.

Briscoe set the pot outside to catch snow falling directly from the sky. He wouldn't do this if they weren't out in the middle of a pristine mountain forest.

When he came back into the tent, Mira was sitting on her sleeping bag, with her laptop perched on her lap, a cord sticking out of it and plugged into a battery pack. Next to where she sat cross-legged, Shiba One was charging as well.

"Who told you to go to Bunker 78?" Mira didn't look up from her screen.

"Why do you ask?"

"Transparency. We're buddies, right?"

"That's the safe house—cabin—where Espy will pick us up."

"Are you sure it's not my dad? It couldn't be Espy, could it? Her history tells me that she rescues as soon as she can. Leaving us to wander around in the forest is not her style."

Briscoe sat down on top of his own sleeping bag. "I haven't worked with Espy much. I don't know how she works. I just assumed she'll come to get us. I wasn't told who will, to be honest."

"You can ask Raynelle Glynn, née Dryden, about the time she was in Italy and needed to be rescued. Espy was right on her tail. Also ask Marie Urquhart, née Bouchard—about the raid in Libya. Espy was on top of it. And ask me about the time we went looking for you in Bitteria. You know how fast she moved to extract Leland, Dario, Iseul, Oliver, and you."

Briscoe said nothing.

"Today her team was at Cabin 109, maybe a few hours ago, and oddly enough nobody came to find us when we're this close to the site. Why is that?"

Some sort of revelation registered in Briscoe's mind. "Good question. Why do you think it's the case?"

"Think about it. I'd like to see your conclusion."

"You don't trust me." Briscoe so wanted Mira to trust him.

"I'm asking to know, not to judge you. I'm trying to list all the possible reasons I can think of regarding why nobody came to rescue us. Instead, they're telling us to hike ten miles to Bunker 78. Don't you find that odd beyond belief?"

"Odd, yes, but not beyond belief."

"Because you know something I don't."

"I was told that Espy is waiting for us and I can find my gear in Bunker 78."

"That's a future that may not happen. All you have is a Glock. It won't protect us. It won't do much to kill Karakurt. I have weapons for you."

"Okay." What else could Briscoe say? He had

taken the gold. Now he had to make good on his promise to deliver Karakurt. Or did he?

"Of course, if we can take her to court, that would be better because then my mother's story will be told to the world. She wouldn't have died in obscurity."

Briscoe frowned at her apparent cold feet. "Do you want Karakurt dead or not?"

"I started out wanting to, but after what happened today, I think justice will be better served in court."

"Thank you." Briscoe had to tell her the flip side of it. "However, if she hurts you in any way, court will be the last thing on my mind."

"If I hadn't been abducted, I'd have shown you what Espy has prepared to let you use."

"Espy?" Briscoe knew that Esperanza had quite a collection of firearms, one for every occasion. At the end of the day, saving lives could be costly. "I thought you didn't trust Espy."

"I have a love-hate friendship with her. She helped me tremendously when we were looking for you in Libya and then in Bitteria. She also came to my rescue in Damascus. If she hadn't airlifted me out of there, I would have died. As it is, I only lost an eye and a hand. However, she's also buddy-

buddy with my dad, so I don't know where her loyalty lies."

"As far as I know, her loyalty lies with God. She seeks the truth in every mission, even now when her Watchfire Security personnel have been compromised. You can be sure she'll get to the bottom of it and she will clean house. Heads will roll."

"You know Espy well."

"Not exactly. We're business associates, not friends, if you ask me. That is to say, we don't hang out or do cookouts. She told me that if not for you, she wouldn't have risked a single person for me in Bitteria. I'm not a valuable asset. Besides, I ended up in Bitteria because of my own doing."

"You sure you went there on your own accord?" Mira looked up. "Or were you forced to go there against your will—cornered into doing something you wouldn't do if you had a choice?"

*Huh.* "What do you mean?"

Silence.

Either she wasn't replying or she was lost in her cyberworld. She typed away on her laptop, muttering to herself.

"Have you turned off your phone?" Mira asked.

"Why?"

"Turn it off. My dad gave you the phone. I'm sure he's tracking you."

"Don't we want to be rescued?"

"Espy can come get us."

"A rescue is a rescue is a rescue."

"Depends on the intention," Mira said. "I want to be rescued sooner than later, and I don't want anyone to thwart an early rescue."

"Are you saying your dad might prevent Espy from rescuing us?"

"If his goal is to use us as bait, he will do his best to help us reach my own mission, which is to track down Karakurt—the real one—and bring justice for my mother. As such, an early rescue would prevent us from carrying out our plans."

It was obvious to Briscoe that Dmitri and Mira both thought their own plans were normal. In their own minds, they had processed information as logically as possible.

Outside looking in, Briscoe couldn't comprehend their method of reasoning that potentially involved deaths. Yet Mira had said before that she'd rather take Karakurt to court. As for Dmitri's methods, he had been used as a tool by both the FSB and the CIA, sometimes in joint operations. According to Tyrone, if Dmitri killed someone, it was state sanctioned.

Right now, Dmitri was after Karakurt, the assassin who'd murdered his wife. Would he sacrifice his own daughter to bring his wife's murderer to justice?

Perhaps it was a good thing that Mira didn't want to have anything to do with her dad—even as she'd freaked out hours earlier when she thought her father had been shot or possibly killed.

Briscoe shut off his Dmitri-issued phone.

While Mira was still busy with her laptop, he sorted out the freeze-dried food in his backpack. "What would you like to eat? Chicken stir-fry? Beef stroganoff? Beef stew? Chicken and dumplings? There's more if none of the above suits your palate."

"I don't care. How do you eat them anyway?"

"I open the bag, add water, stir, and it's ready to eat."

"Huh. Why is there a dampening field in this area?" Mira continued typing. "Looks like I need to find another route."

"What field?" Briscoe poured some water into two packets of randomly picked freeze-dried camping food. They ended up being one beef and one chicken.

"Come see."

Carrying the two packets of food, together with

two sporks he'd cleaned with tissue, Briscoe was about to sit down on his side of the tent when Mira looked up.

"See this." Mira pointed to her laptop screen.

Briscoe sat down next to Mira. "What am I looking at?"

"See the domes that Gauntlet mapped? Points are here, here, here, and so forth. No wonder our texts and phone calls didn't go through."

"It also means no one can call us, right?" Briscoe almost started eating, but he wanted them to say a blessing for the food and ask for God's protection tonight.

"But Ty sent you a text." Mira took the food packet nearest her.

Briscoe ended up with beef. "Assuming he did."

"Oh. Clever." Mira put the food packet next to her on the sleeping bag. "Let's check one more thing."

"Let's say grace first so we can eat."

Mira stopped typing. Picked up her food packet. "What's this?"

"You chose chicken and left me with beef."

She shrugged. "Say grace, Briscoe."

"Father God, thank You for Your sovereignty over all situations, including this one we find ourselves in—perhaps of our own doing, perhaps not," Briscoe prayed. "Give us wisdom to get home safely. Give us extraordinary logic to solve this problem. Give us Your peace about the outcome. Save lives, Lord. Don't let anyone perish without Christ."

"And please show us who the real Karakurt is," Mira whispered.

"Father God, thank You for this food. Provide us clean water. Give us nourishment and a good night's sleep so we can have energy for tomorrow's task ahead of us."

"Make it clear to us whether we should go to Bunker 78 or run super-fast away from it."

Briscoe wanted to laugh, but she was praying seriously. Besides, he agreed with her. "These things we pray in the all-knowing and all-seeing name of Jesus. Amen."

"Amen." Mira turned toward Shiba One on the other side of her. "Shiba One. Wake up."

Shiba came to life. "Yap! Yap! Yap! You rang?"

Briscoe nearly choked on his beef stew. "He speaks?"

"I activated his language module. Kindergarten level, but beats his one-syllable yap response to everything." Mira motioned for Shiba to get closer to the laptop. "Shiba, download your observation in the last twenty-four hours and prepare for software updates."

Mira picked up her packet of chicken dinner. "It's cold."

"Edible." Briscoe had finished his. He waited for her reaction.

"It's all right. I'm still thirsty."

Briscoe crawled on his hands and knees to his backpack and returned with his Nalgene water bottle, though not before pouring a cup of it into another cooking pot. "Drink this. I forgot about the snow I'm collecting outside. Let me get it."

As he retrieved his aluminum camping pot containing freshly fallen snow, he thought about what Mira had said earlier. She questioned the wisdom of hiking ten miles away to a remote bunker—which Briscoe assumed was a fancy name for yet another rustic cabin—when Espy could have easily picked them up here, a couple of miles away from Cabin 109.

Add to that the fact they had been unable to use their cell phones on the trail.

And their reliance on a map that was older than the sinkhole out there.

Something was clearly wrong. Mira had seen it. *Thank God I didn't brush her off.*

All arrows were pointing to Dmitri or someone

close to him masterminding this hiking trip. What awaited them at Bunker 78? A killing arena for Karakurt? Or worse yet, a feeding trough for the Wolves?

The *flight* part of him wanted to recommend they abort the mission.

The *fight* part of him said to head for the show-down at Bunker 78.

When he returned to their tent, Mira's arms were folded in front of her chest, and she didn't look happy. "Look at this, Briscoe."

"Give me five minutes to get a fire going to melt this snow." He thought for a split second. "On the other hand, we don't want Karakurt to detect the heat signature."

"The heat shield is dome shaped," Mira reminded him. "If you put the stove right outside the tent, it's still covered by the shield."

"All right. We'll boil more water once we get to the cabin." He realized he wasn't saying Bunker 78 anymore. Dmitri might have picked him to accompany Mira not because she'd already selected him, but because he had been a soldier. A soldier followed orders to a T.

In this case, he'd been tasked to take Mira to Bunker 78. He would put in his best effort to take her to the rendezvous. That was, assuming he trusted Dmitri's words to be true.

After spending time with Mira, his trust for her father had eroded exponentially. If Mira told him one more thing about Dmitri, Briscoe was sure that his trust for the former spy would melt away like the snow was about to do.

Dmitri had expected to be able to read Briscoe like a book. No surprises.

Well, it seemed that Mira knew him better. Mira had expanded his way of thinking. He could, if he wanted to, be unpredictable.

A contrarian, Tyrone would call such a person.

Would it be unpredictable if Briscoe did not take Mira to Bunker 78?

As the ultralight liquid-fuel stove heated up his cooking pot with a layer of water in it, he slowly dropped clumps of snow into the pot, stirring to melt it.

Thinking, praying, thinking—

"Briscoe! The perimeter alarm went off."

He heard her before she arrived at the tent door.

"Three people coming." Her whispers were loud, but she could barely talk while hyperventilating. "South-southwest. Armed."

"ETA?"

"Five minutes on foot."

Briscoe turned off the stove. Checked his Glock.

"We have thirty seconds to pack our gear and run." He rushed into the tent and zipped up his backpack. Put it over his shoulders. It was lighter now that they had unpacked the tent, self-inflating pads, and sleeping bags.

Mira tossed her laptop, mouse, and battery pack into her backpack. She zipped it up and pulled it over her shoulders.

She started to roll up her sleeping bag.

Briscoe was faster. He rolled up his, snapped the elastic band into place, and did hers too.

Out the door they went, carrying their sleeping bags, a necessity on a snowy night.

He wasn't sure if they had taken thirty seconds or more, but they made it.

For now.

A small virtual screen projected two feet in front of Mira in the dark. Her prosthetic left hand glowed like a flashlight. "North is this way!"

It was as far away as they could get.

They could rush, but they were inside the heat shield that prevented their body heat from showing up on scans.

Mira carried a sleeping bag in her good arm.

She extended her prosthetic hand in front of her, shining on the trail beneath them. Gauntlet guided them forward.

On the virtual screen, Briscoe could see the three red dots behind them, as well as a blinking green arrow pointing in the direction they should go. He and Mira kept moving through the forest, the trail appearing in front of them like magic.

They hiked fast, following the green arrow.

"Where are we going?" Briscoe whispered.

"There's a creek ten minutes away. We go upstream." It was all she said. Her voice sounded nervous, as though this was all new to her.

Having served in various conflicts around the world, Briscoe didn't think rushing through the forest rose to the level of running through sniper fire.

He put his hand on Mira's shoulder. "We'll be fine."

"I had to unplug the laptop midway through the data upload, and it might have caused a problem with Shiba's software."

Oh, she was worried about something else. "Ah, more debugging."

"This shouldn't be an issue on normal days, but he's been through a lot today." Mira sighed. "I'm expecting a lot from him."

"What are you talking about?"

Mira didn't reply.

"I had no idea there was a trail here," Briscoe said as the trail continued.

"Neither did I." Mira almost slipped on the snow mixed with clay.

Briscoe grabbed her arm. "You okay?"

"I'm fine, thanks. This trail should take us to the water. There's a cabin two miles away that we can find shelter in."

"Will they let us in?"

"Well, I picked one that's empty. I've booked it for four nights because that's the minimum requirement, but we'll only stay one or two nights at most. Check-in is at three o'clock, but they'll let us in if it's empty—which it is. I have the code to the door."

"Wait. I thought there was a dampening field in this forest. How did you get on the internet to book the cabin?"

"Well, maybe it's best if you don't know," Mira said.

"What does that mean?"

"It means I was able to access the cabin management website and book us a cabin. Be happy about the end result."

"You thought of everything." Briscoe tried not to show frustration in his voice.

"Not everything. I wanted to check with you first, but I saw the triple dots on the security screen and knew the perimeter had been breached. I had to pay the deposit and close the screen."

"You must type fast."

"I was desperate. Two separate bedrooms, by the way, but no dishwasher."

"A rustic cabin. Then again, roof over our head and probably running water."

"Right."

"Thank you. How did you find that cabin?"

"I superimposed your old map, which I have a copy of on Gauntlet One, onto my terrain photographs, and I came up with this route and that cabin."

"What made you do this?"

"My rule of thumb in robotics is to always have a backup plan or an escape route. Always have a backup plan, I say, but pray you never have to use it. Unfortunately, we do now."

"An escape plan." Now this would be unpredictable.

Mira was out of breath. She stopped talking and simply walked briskly along the snowy path.

Along the way, Briscoe could hear twigs and small branches snap off the trees, falling to the ground—with all the snow on them—with a whooshing sound.

They hiked in silence for a while as snow continued to fall. Soft flakes that looked like they might stick after all and not turn into sleet or ice. Ice would be treacherous to walk on, since their hiking boots were not made specifically for winter hikes on slippery ice.

Briscoe guessed it was very late in the evening, but his phone was turned off, so he couldn't tell the time. "What time is it?"

"Almost midnight."

"We didn't get any sleep."

"If we had turned in early, would we have been able to run from the intruders?" Mira asked.

Briscoe had no answer to that question.

They hiked in silence, slowing down as the trail went uphill.

He was listening to the silence, trying to pick up any unusual noises. Mira still led the way, now walking at a brisk pace. Every now and then she used her gloved hand to hold on to a rock along the trail.

Then he heard it.

*Great. Another drone.*

One, two, then three drones passed overhead.

They spread out, underbelly lights showing Briscoe their formation.

He prayed that their heat shield would hold. If he or Mira slipped on the trail, they would be separated and the heat shield from Mira's backpack would break.

He quickened his pace and held on to Mira's shoulder.

"Drones overhead," he whispered. "Stay together to keep the heat shield intact."

Mira nodded.

"Maybe power down your flashlight?"

Mira tried. The passive light from Eagle Eye's projected screen was too faint to show the path.

She slowed down, clearly unsure where to go.

They came to a natural landing between slopes, where a tree trunk tried to find its way to underground water sources. Part of the tree trunk protruded above a light dusting of snow.

Speaking of snow, it had stopped.

"Maybe we can hide here for a while." Briscoe pointed to the tree.

Mira motioned for him to take the lead.

Their best bet was to hide until danger passed them by. If Mira had a way to shoot down the drones, they'd give away their position.

A predictable reaction was to retaliate.

Or was it to hide?

They sat shoulder to shoulder on a dry tree trunk.

Briscoe prayed there were no critters around them that might scare Mira. As for him, he'd grown up with backyard bugs. While in the US Army, he had spent weeks in a tropical jungle, eating fruits and creatures he'd never even seen before in the name of survival.

Having said all that, it was winter in North Georgia. No bugs or snakes to worry about.

But yeah, if he had to hunt for a squirrel to feed himself and Mira, he could do it—although he'd much rather eat real chicken.

Somewhere in the distance, Briscoe heard at least two gunshots echoing in the forest. He supposed it might have come from their campsite, but he couldn't tell.

"What's that?" Mira leaned toward Briscoe.

"It's all right." No, it wasn't.

Mira wrapped her hands around Briscoe.

"Pray," he whispered, wanting to give Mira something to do.

She didn't reply.

Something whistled past his ears, and Briscoe ducked. He couldn't see in the dark.

"That was a bullet. I think fifty caliber."

*How did she know? Oh, Eagle Eye.*

A sharp pain hit his left shoulder.

A ricochet?

Briscoe grabbed Mira's arm, and he rounded the tree trunk until they were on the other side of the tree, under bushes. No lush leaves here since it was winter, but it would have to do.

He winced.

"We could run," Mira suggested.

How could she think about running out there in the open—whether up or down a trail—in the middle of flying bullets?

Who was shooting at them? Drones?

If the drones were armed, they were clearly illegal—unless this was a government operation. He doubted that because their current problem wasn't related to any government, unless the Russian government wanted a piece of Karakurt as well.

*They can have her, for all I care.*

Tyrone's invitation to be a farmer at Still Waters sounded more and more enticing about now.

Briscoe could hear the drones hovering overhead. Could they be the same drones that had chased Mira and Shiba One earlier this afternoon?

Mira tapped her prosthetic hand. A screen

appeared. She tapped what appeared to be instructions.

Briscoe read the screen.

*Analyzing.*

"What is it doing?" Briscoe whispered.

"Analyzing." Mira didn't elaborate.

What was Gauntlet One analyzing?

The results came. Mira nodded. "Just as I suspected. Same drones from this afternoon."

"I wondered. How did they find us?" Briscoe asked.

"We're on the grid." Mira turned on a low-level beam of a Gauntlet flashlight and slowly moved her backpack from her back to her lap. She reached into it with her right hand while her left hand provided the dim light.

She pulled out two prosthetic hands, which seemed to be her backups. She locked them together in the middle. Now it looked like a bat with two wings. A new virtual screen appeared.

Mira tapped on the virtual keyboard.

All Briscoe could see was a bunch of codes.

"Get your Glock ready," Mira said. "I'm going to deactivate the heat shield for a few seconds so I can release my Glove Drone."

Glock in hand, Briscoe watched as the new

Glove Drone flapped and lifted off like a bird, disappearing into the night.

Mira reactivated the heat shield.

Briscoe had thought that Mira might shoot down the drones, but he doubted the Glove Drone had any firepower.

His next thought was that the Glove Drone carried an EMP detonator. However, it would be a self-inflicted wound because her laptop and prosthetics and wearables would all fry.

His shoulder still hurt. He reached for it under his winter coat, and his skin was sticky to the touch. He guessed that a bullet had penetrated the heat shield and the goose-down filling, hitting him on the shoulder.

It had to be a stray because the enemy drones couldn't have detected their heat signature under the heat shield. Then again, Mira had said the shield was still in test mode.

Slowly the drones motored away.

The night was silent again.

The Glove Drone descended in front of them and returned to Mira. She uncoupled them and returned Gauntlet Two and Gauntlet Three into her backpack.

"Success," she mumbled.

"Success?" Briscoe asked. "What did they do?"

# CHAPTER ELEVEN

Mira sat on the Adirondack chair facing the creek. Between the creek and the house, Briscoe was attempting to chop wood with a slight wound on his shoulder. Mira wondered if he was trying to show off how tough he was, that if he had survived a stray bullet going through his goose-down coat and grazing his shoulder, then surely he could chop firewood.

Fortunately, Briscoe was right handed and the wound was on his left shoulder. So there he was, swinging his ax one handed. Mira wondered if she should go inside the cabin, where she'd be safe behind a log wall.

*Yeah, I better go inside.*

The door creaked as she entered the kitchen. It was cold inside the cabin, so Mira didn't remove her coat.

The kitchen was small. There was a microwave and stove but no dishwasher. Under the sink, there was a half-bottle of dish liquid from the previous renter. Most importantly, the cabin had plenty of running water.

*Thank God for running water.*

The cupboard and refrigerator were bare, as expected. There was no heat. The only source of heat would be the fireplace. Hence the need for more firewood.

Briscoe said that if they ran out, he'd take a walk in the woods and pick up some fallen branches.

Mira sat down at the kitchen table, where her laptop had finished charging.

*Thank God for electricity.*

They had arrived late last night, after hiking in the dark uphill. It had been nice to flick a switch and plug in all their devices to charge up.

By the time Mira had fallen asleep, it felt like dawn was breaking. However, she hadn't slept for long. She had woken up at eight o'clock, starving. Somehow Briscoe must be in tune with her, because he'd also woken up at the same time.

They had picked their bedrooms randomly and couldn't see their window views until morning. It turned out that Mira had the bedroom in the back with the view of the creek, while Briscoe had a view of the front yard and the open field leading to a small waterfall and a gurgling brook.

After a breakfast of more freeze-dried food, Briscoe had gone outside to chop firewood. He said if he was up to it when the weather warmed up, he'd wade in the creek to try to catch some fish for lunch. Either he wasn't worried about the meeting, or Mira had been overthinking.

Mira didn't have time to worry about lunch. The meeting had been scheduled for 1:20 p.m., but it could happen at any time.

And anybody could walk in the front door, except Sinead because she was apparently in jail in Dahlonega, awaiting trial for abducting Mira and falsely imprisoning her. Those were mild acts compared to what Karakurt could really do to her.

Would the real Karakurt show up?

A gamble, Mira's old friend Alicia would say. Mira remembered sitting at Alicia's house, listening to the nonagenarian giving her life advice while trying to sew wearing thick glasses. Every now and then Alicia would stop and ask Mira to help her thread a needle.

Why that memory passed through Mira's mind now, she didn't know. However, she knew that she wanted a laid-back life like that. She had made the right decision buying that cabin in Still Waters and couldn't wait to go home.

Yes, home.

In the meantime, she was close to meeting her mother's killer—or killers.

Mira hadn't asked for the meeting randomly. Based on the data collected by Shiba One on Sinead's super-drones that had carried them away and the drones that had chased them through the woods, Mira found out that these drones would be too expensive for Sinead to afford on her own.

Where had she gotten her funding?

Sinead had to have lied about salvaging the drones from Bitteria. The super-drones were fully operational, indicating that they might have been purchased before the CIA raid. If so, then someone with millions of dollars in cash had paid for the Garuda super-drones, with their proprietary hexagonal formation, from Buchanan Industries.

And Sinead had two sets of those drones.

There was more. Sinead's lodge was listed at eleven million dollars the last time it was sold two years ago. Which meant that Sinead hadn't just dropped in five months before. Who sent her to the United States?

Who paid the salary of her full-time security team? They looked like ex-military, the more Mira thought of it.

Therefore, Sinead must have a benefactor.

Who was this person?

Then there was Oksana Spencer, the woman in Cabin 109. Was that even her real name? Did Dad know the truth about that woman? Was she really retired from the FSB or just taking a break?

Was Sinead right about Oksana being Karakurt, the assassin who killed Mira's mother? Sinead seemed adamant that she had the right person, when everyone on Dad's side said Oksana was apparently just his girlfriend.

Sinead had told Mira that not only was Oksana the real Karakurt but that Dad was her handler. Too bizarre to believe.

If Oksana was the assassin, who had hired her to kill Mira's mother? Surely Dad had not conspired against his own wife. Or had it been a crime of passion, since both women had loved the same man, Mira's dad?

Mira reminded herself what Briscoe had told her, that Esperanza had staged the raid at Cabin

109, using decoys for all three players: Briscoe, Oksana, and Dad. Which meant that Esperanza had agreed with the idea that Oksana was not Karakurt, and for that matter, that Dad was also not her handler from the FSB. Otherwise Esperanza wouldn't have participated.

Esperanza was usually not wrong. Did that mean Mira had to rule out Oksana?

It would break Dad's heart to find out that he was dating his wife's killer.

She remembered what Sinead had told her. Oksana worked for the Wolves. Vitaly was the leader of the Wolves. Therefore, Oksana worked for Vitaly.

In fact, Mira's mother and Vitaly had known each other so well that they'd often visited each other for dinner, even when Dad was away on CIA assignments that sometimes took him deep under-cover for months. Vitaly was like the uncle that Mira didn't have.

Was Vitaly the puppet master?

Mira knew she had to go back to the original premise. She believed that her mother had been killed because she had stolen a list from someone. From whom had she taken the list?

There were four people to choose from: Oksana, Sinead, Vitaly, and Dad.

Who had the most to lose? Who had the most to gain?

Only one person on her shortlist had connections in strong ways with the other three people. With Oksana because she'd been working for him as an assassin. With Sinead since she'd followed Mother around as her assistant and was privy to all of her activities. And with Dad because he was married to the woman Vitaly loved.

It boggled Mira's mind that the person she had known as Uncle Vitaly was actually the leader of the Wolves, an organization that had attempted and failed to overthrow the Russian government.

If that was the truth—if Sinead could be believed—then the message Mira had ordered Glove Drone to deliver the night before would be met with an expected response from none other than Vitaly Zaitsev himself.

Was he in town? Or had he sent the Wolves on their own while he stayed in his various luxurious villas in Europe?

Mira tapped on the Gauntlet logs on her laptop to display the message its backup prosthetics had transmitted to the drones on the other side.

*Leave my dad alone. He'll die eventually of heart problems. You need not worry. Meet me in person*

*at Cabin 120 at 1:20 p.m. to discuss a fair price
for the list.*

Yes, so she'd offered to sell the list to Vitaly—
assuming Vitaly had been the financier behind
Sinead and Oksana both. It made sense since Vitaly
had both means and reputation to do it. His close
ties to Buchanan Industries meant he had been able
to leave Russia and hide somewhere in the world—
perhaps the United States.

If Vitaly showed up, then Mira had hit the jack-
pot. The question then would be if she could
survive it.

If Vitaly didn't show up, then Mira was no
closer to closure than when her nightmare had
begun—when she'd received the news of her mother's death nine years ago in her last year of college.

Mira had only been a teenager when Mom and
Vitaly had struck up a friendship. From what little
interaction she had with the Russian general, Mira
could say that Vitaly had always been a calculating
businessman at heart. He'd negotiate with anyone
for a price.

Therefore, Mira wanted to talk to him about a
potential sale, knowing he'd try to get himself a
deal.

If he showed up at Cabin 120, it meant it wasn't a coincidence that he was in the United States at the same time as Oksana. Had they traveled together?

Perhaps Oksana was Karakurt after all. If she were and she worked for Vitaly, then she'd be after the list as well, as a favor to her employer. The list in question contained the names of seven generals who'd wanted to overthrow the Russian government nine years before.

Vitaly Zaitsev was one of them.

Surely the FSB wanted this list.

So would the CIA.

Mira knew that she could no longer hold on to the list. She wanted to send a copy to her friend in the CIA, Dario de la Cruz, who had helped her track down and rescue Briscoe a year before. Dario was her insurance in case anything happened to her. However, if Dario felt that he had to disclose the list to save lives, then it would put Mira in danger.

Mira decided to send him an encrypted file via a secure channel, then schedule a message to be delivered to Dario in the event that Mira was murdered.

Then she sent a reminder to Leland and Esperanza to stay cloaked because her soon-to-come visitor would most definitely scan the property and surrounding areas. Of course they knew what to do. Esperanza was no spring chicken, but Mira felt better sending the encrypted messages.

While she felt safe that Esperanza was within helicopter range, the latter had argued with Mira about being farther than a bullet could hit Mira first. Briscoe was with her, but they didn't have firearms in the cabin. All Briscoe had was a Glock handgun. Mira asked Esperanza to bring Briscoe a sniper rifle.

Just in case.

And just in case also, Mira had already made a will a few days ago. If she died, all the money in the trust fund her mother had left her would go to Still Waters to be used for safety and protection of its residents, including the elderly who wanted to get away from technology and the children who needed good teachers in their small community school.

Most importantly this morning, she had read her Bible. If it was time to go to heaven, she was ready to go. Dad would be fine because Tyrone's community would take care of him in his senior years.

Mira was at peace except for one thing. She

wished she had married and had kids so that she could pass on Shiba One and her wearables to the next generation so they could improve the technology. Okay, maybe that wasn't the reason to have kids.

Mira chuckled.

A message flashed on her laptop screen.

*Unable to find Shiba One.*

"Try again." She typed new commands, running yet another satellite sweep. "Where are you, little one?"

She had left Shiba at their campsite the night before, telling it to hide in the bushes and observe any new drones. In her hurry, she had forgotten to tell him how long to remain hiding and incommunicado. So he was probably still hiding somewhere in the bushes near the sinkhole.

Now he was missing. Or he'd run out of battery and couldn't call in.

Mira tried one more scan—

The kitchen lights shut off.

Everything went dark in her left eye.

"Uh-oh. Didn't I charge it up?" She remembered rebooting Eagle Eye the night before for maintenance reasons and then charging it while she slept.

With her good eye, she noticed that her laptop had also blacked out.

In the sunlight outside the window, Mira was able to find her phone. It was not working.

She checked her prosthetic hand. The computer did not respond.

She blinked. Eagle Eye did not reboot. She was back to being blind in her left eye. Back to adjusting to seeing with only one eye.

Had someone released an electromagnetic pulse in the area? The EMP would take out all electronics and electricity within the boundaries of the radiation. Mira hoped the radius was small because if Shiba One was outside the range, he could still return.

She unzipped her backpack, a Faraday cage with new experimental anti-EMP lining that VenomLabs was testing. Thanks to Dad—whom she still hadn't reconciled with—she had become a tester for Venom-Labs products, including her prosthetic eye and hands.

That status came in handy now, as she found her tablet still functioning, as were her two backup prosthetic hands. However she had no backup eyeball—which was being upgraded at VenomLabs.

Mira logged on to her tablet and tapped as fast as she could. She had to keep the light on for Shiba

One to find her. She prepared encrypted files for automatic upload to Shiba One once he was within range.

She sent two new messages. Esperanza did not respond, but Leland replied instantly.

**LELAND**

You have a blackout from the creek to the hill behind the waterfall. I'd say two miles in diameter. I can't see who's going in and out of the area.

**MIRA**

The EMP probably took out Espy's choppers as well.

**LELAND**

Yes, her choppers and most of her weapons and scopes are down. I called Tyrone to resupply her team.

**MIRA**

Thank you.

**LELAND**

Their nearest backup chopper is in Atlanta. It would take time to rent a local chopper. Trucks can't get to your remote cabin. She'll have to hike.

It sounded like it could take a long time before help arrived. Even if Esperanza could employ super-drones, those could only carry one person at a time.

Mira started to pray for God's mercy. Her best-laid plan was falling apart. The more she prayed, the more concerned she became about her whole project.

She took off her goose-down coat and folded it over the back of her chair. Then she texted Leland again.

MIRA

My phone is down except for this tunnel you created for tiny texts. Even if Espy gets a new phone, she can't call me and I can't call her.

LELAND

Once Tyrone gets Espy a new phone, I can tell her to text Gauntlet or Eagle Eye.

MIRA

Bad news is that Eagle Eye is down. Now it's only as good as a regular glass eye. My backup eye is still at VenomLabs for updates.

LELAND

Hold on. Let me check something.

While waiting for her technical-support friend to get back to her, Mira wondered why Briscoe hadn't returned to the cabin. After she was done talking with Leland, she would go outside to check on him.

Waiting for Leland only happened whenever Mira needed software updates for her wearables. While VenomLabs had produced them, Binary Systems had provided the software and digital security for the products. The symbiosis wasn't unusual to Mira because she knew that Leland's company would've been absorbed into VenomLabs as its subsidiary if not for Leland and her cousin Cayson's insistence on keeping their entity separate for security reasons.

Before Mira could look out the back windows, Leland texted her again.

LELAND

I see a signal from Gauntlet Two.
Is that what you're wearing?

MIRA

Yes. You can tell VenomLabs that
the backpack works against EMP.

LELAND

Give me a minute and I'll check if
we can redirect what Eagle Eye
can do to Gauntlet Two. What
other wearables do you have in
the backpack?

MIRA

That's all.

LELAND

Then we'd better pray for God's help.

MIRA

Already pre-prayed about it.

LELAND

We can never pray enough.

MIRA

Right. One more thing, Leland. I can't find Shiba One. If I send you my software, could you help me track him? I know it's not a VenomLabs product, but...

LELAND

I'll try. Send me the tracking software.

MIRA

Thank you. I'm hoping that Shiba was outside the range when the EMP hit. He might still be operational.

LELAND

Upload the software to a link I'll send you. I'll see what I can do about finding Shiba for you.

The conversation ended with Mira thanking Leland. She zipped up her Shiba Inu Intelligent Version 3.0 tracking software and was about to upload it when she decided on something better.

She would give Leland developer access to her Shiba communication systems. If Leland could somehow contact Shiba One, then she could direct him back to Mira. That way if Mira was preoccupied at the meeting, Leland wouldn't have to wait for her.

Not only that, Mira sent Leland all the data that Shiba One had collected on the Buchanan drones. Might come in handy.

Then Mira walked outside to inform Briscoe, but before she reached the kitchen, she heard a loud crack from the front of the cabin. She spun around as the front door fell away from its rusty hinges. Standing there within the doorframe was a tall older male.

"Mira," he said.

Mira recognized his voice but not the face. His face was smooth, and parts of his skin looked stretched. His nose was small, and his nostrils flared. His hair was strawberry blond, but it looked more like a wig.

Beside him was a woman who looked like the one Mira had seen on the live feed from Cabin 109. Esperanza had found a great decoy. This one right now must be the original. Dad's girlfriend, whom Mira had never met. Sinead had said that she worked for the Wolves, but Mira had only seen

Vitaly with her mother, never anyone else. All that had been hidden from her.

Oksana Spencer stared at Mira with disdain.

Mira tried to avoid eye contact with her. She looked past Oksana's shoulder to the people behind them, outside the front door. They faced away from the cabin.

Noise from the kitchen made Mira turn her head. Several tall men and women, dressed all in camouflage and heavily armed, filed in from the kitchen to the living room.

In other words, there was no way Mira could get out of here on her own.

*Vitaly and the Wolves are here.*

"I'm your uncle Vitaly." He held out his arms, waiting for a hug.

Mira almost asked what happened to his face but she guessed it was due to plastic surgery. The wig masked his hairline, which had been receding since he'd been in his forties.

Vitaly Zaitsev in the flesh.

"Are you here in the States on a tourist visa?" As soon as Mira asked, she knew it was the wrong question.

"Of course. I have a new passport now from another country."

"Which country?"

"Not for you to know." Vitaly made a show of studying her. "They say you've sort of lost your mind."

"They who?"

"Nobody of sound mind would've posted an 'assassin wanted' request on the dark web. You know how many agencies would be descending on your door?"

"No one came."

"Because it's a crazy request, right? How many candidates did you get?"

"One." Mira closed her eyes. Shouldn't have said a word.

"You mean your boyfriend in the backyard fishing in the stream with his bare hands?" Vitaly raised an eyebrow. His forehead didn't crease. In fact, no muscle around his eyes moved.

"What did you do to him?" Mira's eye flared.

"Tsk. Tsk. Never fall in love with an employee." Vitaly wagged a finger. "It cannot end well."

Oksana stepped toward Vitaly and whispered in his ear.

Vitaly nodded.

"Surprised to see you two together, and yet not too surprised." Mira stared at Oksana. "Does my father know that you work for Uncle Vitaly?"

"You still call him uncle? What are you? Five years old?" Oksana laughed.

Vitaly laughed with her.

"Sinead would be here too, but you put her in jail." Oksana's voice was bitter, as if she perpetually lost everything she tried to do. That kind of bitterness.

"Sinead was looking for my mother's killer, the same as I am, but she abducted me and broke the law." Mira's eyes met Vitaly's. "Promise me you'll leave my father alone and we'll talk."

Vitaly snarled. "Your father killed your mother and got away with it."

Everyone had said one thing or another to Mira. Who could she believe? Who could she trust?

"No, sir. I'm thinking that you or one of your subordinates killed my mother because she stole from you."

Vitaly laughed. "Why would I bother? I don't get my hands dirty anymore. I'm retired."

"You wouldn't have had to get your hands dirty if someone else did the work for you."

"You still have no idea how much your mother meant to me and why it hurt me badly when she betrayed me." Vitaly stared her down from his six-foot-four frame.

How did this seventy-year-old man keep fit and muscular?

"Your mother was the most beautiful woman on the planet, and she made the best custard." Vitaly motioned to Oksana. "She hosted the most lavish parties and introduced me to kings and queens."

Oksana produced two pairs of thick cable ties and tied Mira's hands behind her back.

"Svetlana and I... Those were the days," Vitaly finished.

"What are you trying to tell me?" Mira asked.

"I could've married her, but she chose Dmitri. You could've been my daughter, but you are Dmitri's." Vitaly patted his own chest. "How it hurts in here for so many years, and now I will never get her back."

If Vitaly was in love with Mom, would he have killed her?

Mira began to doubt her own theory.

"All that's in the past now." Vitaly sighed. "I'm tired. I want to retire to Lake Baikal. I've done what I could for Mother Russia. Since Svetlana died, I've lost all interest in politics."

As Oksana tightened the ties around Mira's wrists, Vitaly stepped closer to Mira, so close she could smell whiskey on his breath. For a Russian, he wasn't the vodka sort of guy. Mom had introduced him to whiskey, and they'd gotten drunk together.

That was to say, Mom wasn't the innocent lady in white in all this.

Still, she was Mira's mother, and someone had killed her. Problem was that nobody would fess up to the crime.

"I was going to retire happily, but now I find out that she left you my list, which she stole from me at a party one night." Vitaly got to the point.

Might be why Mira's mother had liked the man. He told her what he thought.

Then again, had Svetlana the spy cozied up to Vitaly only to steal the list?

"Why is the list so important to you?" Mira asked. "Did my mother die so that you can get it back?"

Vitaly frowned. "When you were a teenager, you never asked about anything. You smiled all the time, and you had braces. Now you ask a lot of questions and make trouble for me everywhere."

Everywhere? "This is the first time I've seen you in years, Vitaly."

"Didn't Damascus teach you a lesson?" Oksana spat out the words.

Why would she mention Damascus? "Was it you?"

Oksana ignored her.

"Was it your grenade?" Mira stepped toward Oksana, but two men pulled her back.

"You!"

Again, Oksana did not reply.

"It was meant for your father," Vitaly replied. "Only he had decided to stay home and let his own daughter fall into a trap. I've told him not to mess with Buchanan, but did he listen? Oh no. He had to do his thing."

*Meant for my father?*

Mira found it hard to process.

"What do you think Dad would say if he finds out that his girlfriend was the one who maimed his daughter?"

Oksana's face remained indifferent.

Mira could hardly breathe.

"I'm sure many things have bothered you since you received a posthumous letter from your mother with a safe deposit box key at a bank in Bern, correct?" Vitaly asked.

How did he know about Switzerland? Mira hadn't even told her own dad about it. She had only told one person: Sinead.

Where else could Vitaly have obtained the information? Perhaps his vast human intelligence network might have been able to glean such details.

"Were you keeping an eye on me?" Mira replied with a question of her own.

What was found inside the bank deposit box in Bern, Switzerland, was between Mira and her mother. It was none of Vitaly's business.

True, Mira had casually mentioned to Sinead about her visit to Switzerland. When pried, Mira had simply stated that her mother had left her something that put her on a quest for justice.

Oddly enough, Sinead had never threatened her about the list. In fact, she hardly mentioned it at all. Perhaps Sinead had found the same list independent of Vitaly. After all, she had moved on to other jobs in the industry and had no reason to talk to anyone who was a part of the Wolves.

*Where is Espy?*

Maybe Esperanza and her people were already in the area. Mira prayed that they would rescue Briscoe and give him body armor.

Mira's job was to stall for time and stay alive until help came.

More armed men filed into the small cabin through the front door. They hauled someone in, all beaten up and with clay and mud stuck all over his bomber jacket. He looked in Mira's direction.

Oksana's eyes widened.

Mira ignored her. "Dad! What are you doing here?"

"What are you doing here yourself?" Dad turned to Vitaly. "Let her go. You and I have a long history. She doesn't."

"She has my list."

"The list that Svetlana handed down to Mira did not come from your vault."

"How do you know?" Vitaly asked.

"Because she gave your list to me before she died and told me to do whatever I want with it, so I kept it. It also allowed me to compare the two lists when Mira got hers. They overlap but are not exact matches."

"Wait a minute, Dad. When did you compare your list with mine?" Even though this was a bad time, Mira was truly curious about Dad's connection to the two lists.

"So both of you have a list that overlaps with each other. Great. I want both lists," Vitaly declared.

Dad cleared his throat. "I tell you the truth today. Mira no longer has her list."

"Dad! Did you steal it from me?"

Dad looked at her. "I'm sorry, Mira. I had to protect you. I promised your mother I'd take good care of you. So I am. If you had the list, you'd be in danger. Vitaly will go after you—see what he's doing now? So I took the list from you."

"When?"

"Last week when we had a big fight and you quit working for me as my housekeeper."

"What?" Vitaly looked perturbed. "You made Svetlana's daughter clean your house?"

"And cook too." Mira held her head up high.

"She's a very poor cook. I lost a lot of weight when she cooked. She spent all her time building robots that can flip burgers. Her degree in robotics is totally going to waste." Dad shook his head. "When she quit last week, I threw out her stupid robot."

"Yeah, you did. I saw it in the salvage yard."

"Please, you two. From now on, you don't speak to each other. Only to me." Vitaly breathed deeply. "I never understood why Svetlana chose you over me."

"I'm handsomer than you, I beat you at chess, and I am a superb ballroom dancer, lithe on my little feet." Apparently they hadn't injured Dad's mouth. He could still rattle off words.

"They say that self-praise is no praise," Vitaly said. "Besides, you don't have little feet. You wear size thirteen double-wide shoes."

"Nonetheless, Svetlana married me. So I won."

"But you killed her. So you lost."

"I didn't kill her. I've been looking for her killer since the day she died. I can't find her." Dad's eye was on Oksana.

"I didn't kill her," Oksana said flatly. "I'm here to do a job for Vitaly."

"I thought you came to see me." Dad's voice sounded hopeful at first, and then it sank. "You never worked in Vitaly's mailroom, did you?"

Oksana laughed. "You believed everything I told you."

"So I did." Dad sighed.

"You are part of my job, darling."

"Oh." Dad's face fell, as though pricked by a thousand little needles.

Mira felt sorry for him. Dad hadn't shown emotion like this since his wife died. Tears were pooling in his eyes. Maybe he thought he'd found new love again with Oksana. "Dad, I'm sorry I said you were heartless."

"He is." Vitaly's voice sounded like he believed it himself.

"Mira," Dad said.

Mira wanted to go to Dad, but strong men held her back.

"Mira, we should have worked together to find

closure. We lost nine years due to my own self-ishness."

"Mine too." Mira blinked.

"Let me salvage this father-daughter relationship for you." Vitaly nodded to Oksana. "I'll give you a last chance on earth to work together."

# CHAPTER TWELVE

"I'm claustrophobic," Dad declared.

*No, you're not.*

"If we have to wait, could we wait outside by the waterfall?" Dad asked Vitaly. "Svetlana loved waterfalls. I don't mind dying there."

Mother loved waterfalls? New information to Mira.

"Hmm. She never mentioned waterfalls to me." Vitaly tilted his head.

"Not until she came with me to the United States." Dad grinned like a Cheshire Cat, as though he had finally one-upped his rival. "I've taken her to several waterfalls in Georgia. We went to Anna Ruby and Toccoa Falls, but our favorite was

Amicalola Falls. We hiked from Amicalola to the start of the Appalachian Trail. I miss my Svetlana."

Mira had missed all that because she had been in college, followed by half a dozen years in a robotics career that kept her busy.

It had been sweet of Dad to take his wife on hikes. Perhaps they might have reconciled except for the gulf of separation between them: death.

Mira could hear the waterfall nearby, a grim reminder of their broken family and events that Mira had never been a part of.

Would it have hurt Dad to call Mira and invite her to some of those visits to the great Georgia outdoors?

In the last five years that Mira had worked for Dad, he hadn't gone to a single waterfall. Perhaps this was why.

Vitaly nodded.

Two men in their seventies, each with their own secret thoughts about the same woman. How could that be? Had there been a shortage of women in the world for them to somehow end up loving the same person?

For some reason, Vitaly complied with Dad's request, apparently overtaken by nostalgia.

To the waterfall they went.

Oksana grabbed Mira's hair so hard that Mira

thought she'd pull it out, roots and all. She yelled out in pain.

"Oksana," Dad said in a low tone. "Please don't hurt my daughter."

Oksana didn't look at Dad, but she loosened her grip on Mira.

Slightly.

Outside the cabin and across the unpaved trail, where bits of snow and ice still remained from last night's snowfall, a field of brown grass peppered with snow patches ended at the brook and a small waterfall. The brook cut through a grove of trees, a mix of evergreen and deciduous.

Mira had forgotten where the brook led to on the map, but considering the direction of the water, she would venture to guess that the brook might meet the creek behind the cabin as they flowed downhill.

The creek where the Wolves had found Briscoe.

"Where did you take my friend?" Mira asked Vitaly.

Instead of answering her, Vitaly stared at the waterfall. He wiped a tear from his eye.

If Briscoe had been captured, why hadn't he joined them? Mira guessed that the former soldier had escaped, maybe downstream.

*Fight, Briscoe. Fight!*

"Kneel!" Oksana yelled in Mira's ears, like a drill sergeant.

Mira dropped to her knees, wondering how many decibels had just blasted into her eardrums. Surrounded by unmelted snow, Mira shivered in her sweatpants and sweatshirt.

*God, please let the sun be warm today.*

Next to her, about five feet away, Dad also knelt. His head was down, and in the late morning sunlight, his scalp showed through his thinning hairline.

Dad was growing older right before her eyes.

All things considered, spats between fathers and daughters could happen. But like Briscoe had reminded her on their hike through the woods, she should continue to forgive Dad whenever a painful memory surfaced.

The sound of the waterfall was not loud enough to mask the noise of drones. Mira heard them coming from the eastern and western skies, the fleet converging overhead in a canopy.

Surrounding the probable killing field, Vitaly's armed guards lined the edges of the field, ensuring that no one got in or out. If Mira and Dad were to make a run for it, death was a certainty for both of them.

She could not see Briscoe anywhere, but she assumed he was hiding. If she could see him, so could the Wolves.

*Stay safe, Briscoe.*

"We're going to play a game," Vitaly said. "The name of the game is 'Where's Vitaly's list?' The penalty is death."

"If we produce the list?" Dad asked.

"Earlier you said there were two lists."

"Your game is called 'Where's Vitaly's list?' Technically, we only need to give you one list, and we win."

Oksana nearly chuckled, but her face went back to stoic immediately.

Mira continued to shiver, praying for the sun to rise higher in the sky and warm up the field.

"My daughter's cold," Dad said.

Was he talking to Oksana?

"Please." Dad's voice was quiet. Almost a whisper.

Mira was sure he was directing his pleas to Oksana.

Oksana proved that she had a heart. She asked Vitaly if she could send someone back to the cabin to get coats for Mira and Dad.

"If they don't want to stay out here long, then they can give me my list and the other list."

"If we show them compassion, maybe they will not be so reluctant," Oksana countered. "What's a coat but to cover a dead body?"

Vitaly waved his hand.

Oksana nodded to someone, who jogged to the cabin.

"It's been so long, Vitaly," Dad said. "Why are you still obsessed with the list?"

"Nine years is not long. It's a matter of honor."

"Or dishonor, rather. You plotted against the Russian government. You got away with it. Two of your compatriots did not. It's a matter of time before the other four will speak up against you to save their own lives. You're better off eliminating them than wasting your time chasing a list with names you already know."

"The list was written with our blood," Vitaly said. "Our DNA proved we were together. That, I cannot have."

Mira tried not to react. She knew right away that she did not have that particular list written in blood. She had a printout of something else. Seventeen names.

Perhaps Dad had been telling the truth when he said that Mira's mother had given him a list as well.

"You should've thought of that before you

made that blood pact and whatnot." Dad's voice was calm, as if having a conversation with a friend.

"Whatnot? Why are you taking this so lightly? Are you no longer Russian?"

"Having Russian heritage doesn't mean that I want a resurrection of the czars. It's a new world, Vitaly. And no, Svetlana was never a Romanov— even though she was half-English and half-Russian. Does that answer all your questions?"

*What's all this talk about czars and Romanovs?* Mira found their conversation increasingly bizarre.

"My hands are clean." Vitaly splayed them as he walked around Dad.

"Because someone else cleaned them for you."

Mira didn't know when the coat came, but she turned toward Oksana when she threw a coat over her. Oksana didn't look at her. She went back to her position, standing between Mira and Dad, holding what looked like a Ruger that had probably seen action.

Mira wouldn't have known what make the handgun was if not for Dmitri's collection at the farmhouse.

The coat was warm, and it turned out to be Mira's own gray coat. Unfortunately, whatever electronic devices she'd had in her pockets had all been fried by the EMP. Besides, her hands were literally tied.

Oksana covered Dad with a blanket, and she did it so gently that Mira wondered if she had real feelings for Dad after all. Dad thanked her, as if they weren't surrounded by the Wolves.

Mira couldn't read the unwritten missive that hung between them, but Dad's face showed disappointment.

Perhaps he really hadn't known that Oksana still worked for Vitaly.

Mira's one good eye squinted in the morning sun as she studied Oksana. She was wearing black leather from head to toe, and she carried two sidearms around her waist, plus a dagger of some sort. It had an old carved handle, maybe ivory.

If Eagle Eye were operational, Mira could identify it better. She blinked.

Nothing.

Blinked again.

Still nothing.

Somewhere at the back of her mind, she wondered if her eye socket could have protected Eagle Eye from the EMP blast. Also, the eyeball was small. Perhaps it could escape the radiation.

If so, when could Mira expect Eagle Eye to function again?

No idea.

"Warm enough?" Vitaly asked. "Now the game is very simple. Dmitri said that he has both lists. Fine. So my people will take him to retrieve them."

"That's easy." Dad smiled.

His face was all black and blue and bloody, but Mira could see the smile. Dad had done it for her, she was sure.

"If they do not come back in two hours, then I will carve out her other eye." Vitaly pointed at Mira.

Mira felt a round metal on her head. Sitting on top of her head. It felt like a muzzle. She dared not move, but she knew that Oksana was standing close to her. It was probably her Ruger.

Mira blinked.

*Blink blink blink.*

*Come on, Eagle Eye. You can do it.*

Mira prayed that Leland had tracked down Shiba One somewhere in the forest out there. She also prayed that Vitaly would not ask her if she had backup copies of the list that her mother gave her.

She'd have to say yes.

*Espy, where are you? Please rescue Briscoe.*

Yet again.

Mira watched two men pull Dmitri to his feet. "Dad!"

He turned toward Mira. "Don't worry, sweetie. I'm just going to the farmhouse. I don't know how long it will take, but I don't expect to be gone all day. Wait for me."

Mira nodded as a helicopter came over the trees and descended on the grass and snow. Three men taller and bigger than Dad escorted him to the chopper.

It lifted off before Mira remembered to pray.

Someone brought Vitaly a chair from the cabin. He ordered them to put it next to Mira. "So that we can watch the livestream together."

Twenty minutes after the chopper had taken off, it landed at the backyard of Dad's farmhouse. That told Mira that their cabin was about fifty miles away from the farmhouse.

Two people disembarked from the chopper and ran toward the house. Dad must've given one man the key, because he entered it easily. Ten minutes later they came out.

Mira guessed that they had swept the house and found no one else inside.

One of Vitaly's escorts carried a body camera, which now showed the entourage walking toward the farmhouse.

"I remember putting the lists in my safe." Dad led the way to his home office down the hallway from the dining room, but the lists were not in his safe.

"Ah, I think I put them somewhere upstairs. I was in such a hurry." Dad touched his head. "Also, your people kicked me in the head, so now I'm having a hard time remembering things."

Mira was familiar with the layout of the house but was not surprised that Dad had taken them to various rooms, looking for the lists.

Which might not be at the farmhouse after all, knowing Dad.

"Doc said my memory is going." Dad looked the part onscreen.

Mira began to cry.

"Keep searching," Vitaly barked.

At least that was what Mira thought he did: bark.

Which in turn reminded her of her missing Shiba One.

*Where are you, Shiba?*

The entire upstairs exhausted, Dad went downstairs. "I remember now. I put the lists in a honeypot in the cellar."

Honeypot.

A lightbulb flashed in Mira's mind.

*Honeypot* was a computing codeword for a trap.

*Clever, Dad. Clever.*

Did Dad have any list at all?

*Oh, Dad, you don't need to be my hero. I'd rather have you alive.*

He had gone to the cabin in the woods, either alone or with Esperanza, to keep Mira company and to buy time for Mira's rescuers to get there.

Esperanza moved fast overseas, but this was the United States of America, where a rescue operation like this would require involvement from not only the local police and the Georgia Bureau of Investigations but also federal agencies such as the Department of Homeland Security and the Federal Bureau of Investigations interested in foreign persons of interest.

Such as a wanted man or woman.

The cabin Mira had rented was in a state park. Vitaly, Oksana, and all their merry people had brought firearms to a state park. Now he was turning a vacation cabin compound into an execution ground.

Did they have a concealed-carry permit like Briscoe had?

Watching Dad take Vitaly's men on a tour of his cellar was stressful for Mira because she knew it had to come to an end.

Oksana still trained the barrel on Mira's head. It was unnecessary.

"Uncle Vitaly," Mira said.

"Yes?" Vitaly crossed his leg.

"My legs hurt kneeling like this. How about I sit cross-legged?"

Vitaly shrugged. Oksana lifted her handgun off Mira's head. Mira decided not to complain about the barrel on top of her head. It might be asking too much.

Oksana's arms probably felt tired, so she simply pointed the weapon at Mira. At least there was no contact.

Mira wondered how fast it would take a bullet to leave Oksana's Ruger and hit her, some two feet away.

Drones continued to hover overhead and circled the air like vultures. The sky was clear. The sun rose and warmed up the brown grass. Almost all the snow had melted.

The temperature still felt like it was in the thirties. Mira's coat warmed her up a bit, but her hands and face were cold.

She felt tired. In three days, she hadn't slept much—no more than four hours.

Her stomach growled.

"Your papa better hurry up, or you won't have lunch." Vitaly laughed.

*Where is Briscoe? Espy? Tyrone? Anyone?*

Some yelling caught Mira's attention. She turned toward the noise. One of the perimeter guards was down on the ground. Out cold. Another was hitting something at his knee with the back of his rifle.

"What's going on there?" Vitaly asked.

Everyone looked.

"Yap! Yap! Yap!"

*Oh.*

"Looks like you found my dog," Mira said.

*Thump.*

The guard went down like a felled tree.

Someone pointed his weapon at Shiba One but didn't shoot because the robot dog was attached to someone's ankle.

"Nooooo!" Mira jumped up, and Oksana knocked her down to the ground.

Mira looked at Vitaly. "He's a robot, but he's still my dog."

Vitaly lifted his arm. "Let it go."

"It's tasering everyone. We can't shoot at it because we might take out Bob's arm too."

"Bring it here." Vitaly looked concerned. To Mira, he said, "What's his name?"

"Shiba." Shiba was covered with mud and still hadn't found his fourth leg.

"That's a woman's name."

"You meant Sheba, as in the Queen of Sheba," Mira explained. "This is Shiba, as in Shiba Inu, an ancient Japanese dog breed."

"He has a Taser," one of the guards said.

"Let him stay near me," Mira said.

"Shut it off."

"Okay." Mira ordered Shiba One to go to sleep instead of powering down completely. No one seemed to pick up the difference.

On the projected screen in front of Vitaly, Dad waved a piece of thick paper in the air. It looked like a scroll, and Dad showed the printed side to the camera.

"What makes you think my men wouldn't just kill you right away?" Vitaly asked.

"Because of course, I have backups. Insurance, you know? Release my daughter, and I will give you the other list."

Vitaly nodded to Oksana. She pulled Mira to her feet and moved into camera range. Then she pointed the Ruger at Mira's temple.

"Don't, please!" Dad pleaded.

While Mira was afraid for her life, she could see the look on Dad's face. He showed no fear. Something was up. Dad had a plan.

The day before, she hadn't wanted any help from Dad. Now, Mira didn't care whose plan it was. As long as she, Dad, and Briscoe went home safely, it was all she prayed for.

Quietly, Mira prayed.

Without warning, Eagle Eye came alive. Then it blacked out again. Mira was unable to control it. It flickered on and off. She blinked and closed her eyes just in case Vitaly or Oksana saw it.

When she opened her eyes, Eagle Eye projected a screen two feet away from her nose. The screen was scrambled.

Mira closed her eyes.

"What was that?" Vitaly asked.

"Her prosthetic eye," Oksana said.

"Didn't the EMP take out all electronics?"

"Yes, we thought."

"Take out her eye," Vitaly ordered.

*What?*

Mira opened her eyes. Blinked. The screen went away. "It's gone now."

"Remove her eye and destroy it," Vitaly ordered. "I don't want any communication breach."

Oksana dropped Mira to the ground on her knees again. She put her weapon on the grass. Then she yanked Mira's hair back, held it tightly with one hand, and with the other hand she tried to pry Mira's prosthetic eye out of the socket.

"Wait. Did you even wash your hands?" Mira asked.

Oksana pulled her hair back harder.

Mira winced. Her eyelids held the prosthetic eye, not letting it come out.

"Let me do it myself," Mira pleaded. "I can pop it out in no time at all. I'll hand it to you."

Oksana looked at Vitaly, who nodded. She released Mira's hair.

"My hands are tied behind my back."

Using her dagger, Oksana cut off the cable ties, then pointed the dagger at Mira's neck.

"I need to reach into my coat pocket for a packet of hand wipe," Mira said. "Front right."

Oksana retrieved the packet of wipes for her.

Mira cleaned her fingers and then removed her prosthetic eye, which she handed to Oksana.

At that moment Shiba One woke up and started barking.

"Yap! Yap! Yap!"

He bounced up and down and rolled on the ground.

"No way a robot dog can go rabid," Vitaly said.

In the sky, drones stopped encircling, stalled, and dropped to the ground almost all at once.

*Whoa.*

Who brought down the drones?

Mira glared at Shiba One.

Did Leland reprogram him?

"What's going on?" Vitaly jumped out of his chair. "What did you do to my drones?"

"Yap! Yap! Yap!"

Just like that, Shiba pounced on Vitaly and bit his ankle.

Vitaly convulsed and went down.

Several guards hit Shiba with the back of their weapons. Shiba One released the ankle and ran off. The guards tried to awaken Vitaly.

"Get him to safety. Now!" Oksana ordered.

Mira wondered if she was second in command after all.

They carried Vitaly away, leaving Oksana with Mira. Oksana pulled Mira close to her chest, making her a human shield. "I die, you die."

They backed away.

Moving made them a difficult target for Esperanza to hit. So Mira tried to slow them down by dragging her feet on the ground.

Oksana pulled her up and repeatedly hit her head and shoulders. "Stop stalling, or I will deal with you the same way I took care of your mother."

Was that a confession?

"Are you Karakurt?"

"I don't use that name anymore." Oksana

dragged Mira by the neck. Her elbow pressed against Mira's windpipe, and she started to choke.

Oksana barely loosened her elbow.

"Did you kill my mother to get Dad all to your-self?" Mira asked.

"I had orders. Nothing personal."

"But you benefit."

No reply.

"Yap! Yap! Yap!"

Here came Shiba One trying to bite Oksana's ankle, but she was wearing black boots. Shiba leapt up to get to her knee, but Oksana swatted him away—letting go of Mira in the process.

*Zing!*

Mira heard it before Oksana collapsed to the grass.

"Run, Mira. Run!"

Briscoe's voice.

*Run in which direction?*

Mira had no idea. She ran away from Oksana toward the cabin. She heard a blast behind her and covered her ears as she tripped on the grass and went tumbling. She stretched out her palms to stop the fall.

From the corner of her eye, she spotted Briscoe in a Kevlar vest, holding what looked like a sniper rifle, running alongside Esperanza toward Oksana and Vitaly.

People shouting and loud yelling droned out the sound of the waterfall in the distance.

"FBI!"

"DHS!"

Mira lay flat on the ground, covering her head with her arms and screaming...

Until a strong hand shook her shoulder. "Mira? Mira, it's okay now."

*I'm waking up now. It was all a dream.*

She opened her eyes. Her nose was in the grass and soil. Someone helped her to sit up.

"The EMT is coming, and they'll check you out. Make sure you have no injuries."

The voice was calm and familiar.

Mira looked up to find Briscoe putting his rifle on the ground and reaching for her. She burst into tears.

"I'm sorry I left you alone in the cabin. They found me at the stream, and I managed to get away." Briscoe stroked Mira's back. "When I reached the woods behind the cabin, Espy's people were all over it. They told me that an EMP was deployed."

Mira grabbed his arm. She still didn't look at him. "My dad is at the farmhouse."

"I know. Don't worry. Ty's got it."

"Call him."

"Okay. This is a new phone from Espy." He called Tyrone. "Hey Ty. Mira's safe. Good, good. I'll tell her."

"Your dad's been rescued."

"Thank God." Mira refused to meet his gaze.

"Mira?"

"What?" Her head still down, Mira wanted to ask many questions of her own, but she couldn't get any word out.

"Look at me," Briscoe said gently.

"No."

"Why?" His head was down at her eye level. She closed her eyes.

He seemed to sense why as he held her hands. "Are you a child of God?"

"Yes."

"Then you're beautiful. Period."

"They took my eye."

Briscoe gently pushed strands of hair from her face. "Mira?"

"Yeah?"

"Close your eyes."

"Why?" Mira had to know.

"Close your eyes, and you'll find out."

Mira did and immediately felt soft lips on hers. They were warm against the winter breeze.

She could hear the buzz of activities all around them, but suddenly they seemed to pause, as though to give Briscoe and Mira their moment in the winter sun.

Briscoe pulled back.

"What did you do that for?" Mira asked.

"To distract you from your eye."

Mira shrugged. "It didn't work."

"I guess I need to try harder." Briscoe lifted Mira's chin.

*Take two.*

Mira felt warm all over.

This time it worked.

# CHAPTER THIRTEEN

Three months after Vitaly and Oksana had been extradited to Russia to stand trial for the murder of Svetlana Proskouriakova, Briscoe hadn't left Still Waters even though the weather had warmed up. This was the longest time he'd stayed in one place, but only because he couldn't leave Mira.

He continued to work in the security department of the community, with Tyrone encouraging him to apply for a permanent position. He felt good about being able to protect the people he cared about, especially the person he'd been dating since their forest adventure.

Mira impressed Briscoe when she'd deeded her land around Still Waters to the community free of charge in the memory of Alicia, the deceased charter resident who had been a mother or grandmother to everyone.

Speaking of Alicia, Mira's dad bought her cabin. Briscoe had wanted to bid on the cabin because then he would be Mira's neighbor, but he decided to continue renting a room from Tyrone.

That way if things didn't work out with Mira, Briscoe could just pack his bags and leave. No property to hold on to or to sell. And if things worked out, then perhaps he'd marry Mira and they'd build a log cabin together or expand the one that Mira already owned.

On this clear morning after an overnight rain in the colorful month of April, he had just finished breakfast at the community center. He had packed a to-go breakfast box for Mira and was on his way to the Still Salvage barn to feed his girlfriend pancakes, eggs over well, and bacon on the side.

Mira had been up all night updating software for the two hundred and fifty Shiba robots. The last two holdover programmers at the Atlanta office had joined them at Still Salvage. The city dwellers were still adjusting to life in the countryside, but they did their best to accommodate their employer, who now owned a majority of the shares of Still Salvage.

In fact, Mira had moved her Shiba Inu Intelligent laboratory from Atlanta to Still Waters. She created a new branch of Still Salvage, calling it Still Labs, where they would test wearable computers.

All that meant Mira would be staying in Still Waters for the foreseeable future.

It made it easier for Briscoe to make his own career decisions if he could work around her schedule and plans.

Rounding a grove of flowering azalea bushes, Briscoe was almost run over by three Shiba Inu robots. They looked like the dogs that Mira had let Havilah and Asher debug back in January.

Briscoe wondered whether they'd ever be like Shiba One. Back in January, when Leland had tracked down Mira's lost Shiba One, she'd brought it to their showdown cabin and remotely taken over Shiba's onboard software to attack Vitaly's drones, shutting them down and crashing them to the ground.

"Aarrgghh! I warned you!"

He could hear Mira's voice in the distance.

"I double warned you!"

Briscoe stepped aside to let the three robot dogs and their angry owner pass. He wasn't sure if Mira saw him. He watched in amusement as Mira chased after the dogs—

Straight toward the lake.

One by one they ran onto the boat dock, took a flying leap, and plunged into the lake.

"Oh no you don't!" Mira kicked off her shoes and ran after the dogs.

Briscoe's jaw dropped at the same time the insulated tote in his hand dropped to the ground.

"Stop!" Briscoe's voice rode in the wind, but Mira ignored him.

He knew he could outrun Mira, but it would be close. He picked up his pace and pulled her back from the dock with such a force that he lost his balance and fell back onto the grass.

It was a soft landing, as the ground was still spongy from the rain.

Mira landed on top of him, her elbow on his rib cage.

She rolled off him. She was out of breath. "Briscoe."

"Yes, ma'am?" Briscoe faced the blue sky with tiny puffs of clouds here and there.

"That's two hundred thousand dollars' worth of equipment at the bottom of the lake."

"Not my fault. Write better software, I suppose." Briscoe stood. "You can always dredge out the dogs, but I don't want to have to dive after your dead body."

"You're just being dramatic. You forget that

Eagle Two can see underwater. I would have known where to find the three dogs."

"I forgot you recently had an upgrade on your eye." He pulled Mira to her feet.

They were both covered with soil and mud. They chuckled and stared at each other, as if sharing the same memory.

Briscoe was thinking about their cabin adventure some fifty miles north of here, at the Georgia-North Carolina border. Had it been three months?

"I'm still amazed that you took down Karakurt, but you didn't kill her," Mira said.

Yes, they were thinking of the same life event.

"To tell you the truth, I missed. My hands shook so badly because I thought I was going to hit you too," Briscoe admitted. "Both of you were moving, and I did the best I could. I was also out of practice."

"Then God gave you a miracle."

"Indeed He did."

"Amen," a third person said. A woman's voice.

Briscoe and Mira both turned to see who it was.

"Sinead!" Mira ran to the FSB agent and took her hands.

Sinead Jones—not her real name—was slightly taller than Mira and older by twenty years. The first time Briscoe had seen her was at the mountain cabin.

After escaping Vitaly's people, Briscoe found himself in the forest with Esperanza's team. Before they could finish their battle plans, DHS and FBI arrived, along with Sinead Jones, who had introduced herself as an undercover FSB agent working alongside DHS to take down the Wolves.

Briscoe followed Mira and shook Sinead's hand also. "What brings you to Still Waters?"

"To say goodbye. My cover is blown. I'm finally going home." Sinead blew a sigh of relief. "My kids are teenagers now, and I've missed most of their childhood, including their violin and piano recitals, birthdays, and holidays."

Deep undercover had its pros and cons, as Mira's parents had also found out. Briscoe was glad that Mira could reconnect with her father and make up for the days gone by. He hoped that Sinead would be able to do the same too.

"You never forget your own mother," Mira said. "I'm sure your kids would love to see you home."

Sinead nodded. "I've enjoyed all the years working for your mother as her personal assistant and then the next nine years undercover in your country, looking for her murderer. Your government is very gracious, and I cannot say enough good things about the DHS, who kept my identity a secret."

"You did find Karakurt, after all. Good job." Briscoe gave her two thumbs-up.

"Couldn't have done it without you two—and Dmitri, even though he was a victim of Karakurt."

Mira stepped forward, then stopped. "May I hug you?"

"Sure. No need to ask for permission. I've known you since you were a teenager."

"Well, I wasn't sure if you were carrying a concealed weapon. I didn't want it to go off." Mira hugged Sinead.

Briscoe looked on, wondering how Mira's brain processed information. He supposed he'd have to put up with her.

"Thank God you're not the assassin." Mira let Sinead go. "Otherwise I would have no choice but to ask Briscoe here to shoot you."

"He might miss again, so I think I'll be all right."

Briscoe didn't know whether to feel embarrassed or just grow a thick skin in two seconds. Yes, he had only injured Karakurt, not kill her.

"I still don't fully understand you the way I understand your mother." Sinead held Mira's hands. "When you first asked Briscoe to track down and take out Karakurt, what were you thinking?"

"Briscoe is the only person I trust," Mira said. "Truth be told, at the back of my mind, I knew that the right thing to do was not to kill Karakurt—as in 'an eye for an eye, a tooth for a tooth,' per the Bible —but to take her to court. I was hoping that somehow Briscoe would cut through my fog of grief and help me sort it out before it was too late."

"In a way, he did...by missing." Sinead laughed.

"You'll never let it go, will you?" Briscoe sighed.

"I need stories to tell my grandchildren."

"Then tell them that Mira was held hostage and her life was in danger. At that point, my personal intention of not killing went out the window." Briscoe looked at Mira.

Mira nodded. "By the grace of God, we're still on the right side of justice. If Briscoe had gone through with my crazy plan, we'd be criminals."

"You trusted Briscoe's conscience more than your own." Sinead's voice turned grave. "The fact that you thought I could have been the assassin..."

"You played your role so well that I couldn't tell you were undercover. That day when we went to Cabin 109..." Mira's voice trailed off. "I was so scared of you."

"We had to rattle Karakurt's cage, even though

we knew those three people were decoys." Sinead glanced at Briscoe. "The real Karakurt wasn't going to show herself unless we made it look like we knew who she was. We were right. Only took us nine years to be right."

"You were very convincing. I thought you were really a personal assistant."

"I was before I was recruited by the FSB."

"Oh, I see. They knew you're a natural at details and keeping up with schedules and so forth."

Sinead nodded.

"Maybe your next career could be as an actress," Mira suggested. "You sold me on moving to England, raising chickens in the countryside, and adopting an orphan."

"I'm sorry. I needed a story to flesh out my character. But that's the extent of it. No stage for me." Sinead shook her head. "Once I go home, my family and I will have to move to a place where nobody knows us. We'll have to start over for safety."

"You were good to my mother."

"She was good to me. I went to church with her."

Mira nodded.

This wasn't the time for Briscoe to say that

going to church wasn't enough, and he had no idea whether Sinead was a Christian.

He was glad that they had such happy memories of Mira's mother. Nobody had looked into whether Svetlana ever had an affair with Vitaly before she'd stolen his list.

"I miss your mother. Such an unnecessary death." Sinead's phone pinged. She checked her text, then put away the phone. "Thank you for the list."

"I had a different list."

"For a different mission that someone else will undertake." Sinead smiled. "Our operation paid off. We were looking for the short list of names. Turned out your father had it. As a bonus, you gave us a totally different list that we didn't know about."

"I gave it to the CIA," Mira reminded her.

"They gave it to us after checking to make sure there were no Americans on the list."

Briscoe saw Mira's eyes widen, as though she hadn't thought of that possibility. Neither had Briscoe. The world of espionage was not his realm. He preferred easier, less mentally taxing work. Like patrolling Still Waters and making sure nobody broke into the community.

Mira sniffled. "I'm going to miss you, Sinead—and I guess I will never know your real name."

"No."

"There are a few things that still bother me," Mira said.

She had told Briscoe about it, but he had no answers either. It was fortuitous that Sinead had paid them a visit today.

"If I can answer them, I certainly will." Sinead waited.

"How did you possess Buchanan drones?" Mira asked.

"Confiscated in Bitteria, just as I told you."

"Speaking of Bitteria, it all makes sense now." Briscoe nodded. "I had wondered for one year how you knew that I was in Bitteria. If not for you, Mira wouldn't have paid for my rescue."

"I wouldn't know where to look," Mira added. "Thank you, Sinead."

"No need to thank me repeatedly." Sinead laughed.

Briscoe raised his hand. "Why send the super-drones to pick up Mira? You scared all of us."

Sinead reached for Mira's good arm. "Sorry about that. We had to create some drama to draw out Karakurt. We knew she had arrived in the vicinity earlier than our intel told us."

"She was early by a day." Mira was deep in

thought. "Is that why you abandoned our original plan?"

"Yes. I wanted to protect you from danger." Sinead didn't hesitate answering her. "I lost Svetlana. I wasn't going to lose you too. When we learned that not only was Karakurt in Georgia, she had also made her way to your dad's farmhouse in Dahlonega, I got worried."

"So it was a good thing that I quarreled with Dad last week and moved out," Mira said.

"Actually, I think he made sure that your fight ended up that way. He wanted you out of the house."

"Oh." Mira blinked a few times. "That explained why Ty was so protective over me at Still Waters. He probably talked to Dad. Hmm. All that tells me that Dad suspected Oksana was Karakurt."

Sinead shrugged. "I can't tell you."

Mira rephrased her question. "Did Karakurt confess?"

"She hasn't told us anything yet. For nearly two months, her jaws were wired shut thanks to Briscoe here because he missed a head shot."

"Technically, her jaw is a part of her head." Briscoe bristled. "Then again, Romans 8:28, ladies. If I hadn't missed, Karakurt wouldn't get her day in court."

"Now she's lawyered up, and FSB wants her back in Moscow."

"To stand trial?"

"To help them investigate some cases involving the Wolves."

When Briscoe's eyes widened, Sinead raised her hand. "Don't worry. We'll make sure she pays for all the murders she has committed. Svetlana wasn't the only person she killed."

That made Briscoe feel better about justice systems in Russia, and for that matter, around the world.

"Thank God you didn't kill anyone after all." Mira squeezed Briscoe's hand.

Briscoe smiled. He had tried to return the ten million dollars in gold to Mira for failing his end of the bargain, but she'd refused it. Said he could do whatever he wanted with his paycheck.

After tithe and taxes, Briscoe decided to invest back into Still Waters. The community could use new water pipes, an updated community kitchen, and better security to prevent other drone attacks.

As for the ten million dollars that Dmitri had paid him, Briscoe felt that he'd earned every dollar of it. He had protected Mira all the way, as promised.

In fact, he was still protecting her today.

Mira turned back to Sinead. "Did Dad give you a hard time about using the super-drones? They've been known to drop people from the air."

"It was risky, but we couldn't tell your dad or you. You played along very well."

"I was genuinely scared."

At this point, Briscoe wrapped his arms around Mira's shoulder.

Sinead showed no emotion on her face. "Did you have more questions?"

"The lodge," Mira said. "Your agency must be super rich."

"That incredibly large lodge was courtesy of DHS. Your government is very generous. They were determined to get the assassin out of the country to protect your citizens."

"Our tax dollars at work." Mira nudged Briscoe's side.

"Note that I didn't tamper with your wearable devices while you were napping even though I could have. We also did not put any sleeping pills in your food to make you sleep for longer while we reprogrammed your eye and hand."

"And dog."

"No." Sinead made a face. "I stay away from yapping robot dogs."

"What I'd do." Briscoe pointed to Mira. "She just lost three in the pond."

Mira's shoulders sagged. Then her one real eye brightened, as it usually did when she had an idea or thought. "Final question."

"Yes?" Sinead seemed to be the epitome of patience.

Briscoe supposed that undercover agents had to be that way because sometimes it took a long time to complete their missions.

"When I was at the DHS lodge, why did you prevent me from contacting anyone?" Mira asked.

"Once you contacted Still Waters, your dad would know, and thereby, Oksana—a.k.a. Karakurt —would also know."

"You didn't know for sure that she was Karakurt, did you?"

"My sources said she might be. We had to take a step of faith." Sinead straightened her shoulders, as if saying that the worst was over and she had been proven right. "After nine years of hunting, I was a bit tired, to tell you the truth."

"I'm still stunned that she was dating Dad behind my back," Mira said. "That was news to all of us."

"She kept her enemy close," Briscoe added.

"How long... I mean, I guess I don't need to pry."

"Dmitri told us everything about their relationship, but it's in confidence." Sinead looked sad. "I'm afraid I cannot tell you now or ever."

"Maybe I don't want to know."

"Ignorance is bliss." Sinead chuckled.

"Was their relationship also why you didn't come after me at Cabin 109 when I bolted from you?" Mira asked.

"I had to let you go because I didn't want to turn the spotlight on my team. We were clearly not from the Wolves. If Karakurt put two and two together, she might have ended up spelling FSB. We couldn't have that."

"The forest had a cell phone dead zone," Briscoe said. "Was that your doing?"

"Wasn't me." Sinead sounded genuine. "Maybe it was really a dead zone."

Briscoe thought her eyes twinkled, but it was fleeting, and he had no proof beyond his own observation.

Sinead received another text. "This time I have to go. Sorry. I'd love to chat with you, but I have a flight to catch."

Briscoe put his arm over Mira's shoulder to

provide her with emotional support. "Hate to say goodbye, but we will never see you again, will we?"

"No. I can't even attend your wedding." Sinead put away her phone.

"What wedding?" Mira asked.

Briscoe had no idea either. It might be too soon to propose to Mira, considering they had only dated for three months—even though Mira had loved him for three years.

"In any case, I think your friend Leland knows how to track me down. If you ever get into trouble again, call me."

"I hope she stays out of trouble," Briscoe said.

"However, give me a few years, okay? I need to rest and enjoy my family for a while. I don't need any wild drama to upset my retirement." Sinead looked relieved.

"Let us walk you to your vehicle," Briscoe said.

"How nice to have a security escort." Sinead followed Briscoe.

Mira caught up to Sinead. "It's hard to let go of friends."

"We'll always be friends in our hearts." Sinead's voice cracked.

Mira and Sinead were arm in arm as they walked to the entrance of Still Waters. Briscoe stepped back and walked behind them, checking his phone for messages from Tyrone.

He remembered the breakfast he'd dropped near the lake just before his attempted rescue of his girlfriend from certain impulsive diving. He'd have to go back and pick up the insulated tote or be accused of littering.

Sinead entered an SUV with a diplomat tag. Briscoe and Mira waved until the vehicle disappeared around a bend on the road.

Mira hugged Briscoe and cried. "So many people from my past are gone."

"I'm still here!" someone yelled.

Dmitri's voice was loud, and it echoed in the morning.

He was getting out of his truck. He went around to the other side and opened the passenger door for...

Ailey.

The resident RN at Still Waters.

She waved to them and disappeared down the sidewalk toward the community clinic.

How quickly Dmitri had moved on from Oksana.

"We just came from the farmhouse," Dmitri said to Mira and Briscoe.

"We don't have to know," Mira said.

"She wanted to see the chickens." Dmitri looked like he wanted to explain. "And goats."

Briscoe nodded. "Glad you could give her a tour of your farm."

"She's helping me with nutrition. I'm trying to eat healthy, considering I need to lose the weight I've gained the last three months eating the good food here."

"I'm glad you're eating healthy, Dad."

Briscoe was proud of Mira for not getting upset that her dad had started to eat well—after he'd stopped eating what her robots cooked at the farmhouse.

"Say, I know I said I wanted to retire, but do you happen to have any computer job I can do at Still Salvage?" Dmitri asked.

"Are you really retiring if you still keep your Prague office?"

"I'll fly there to work from time to time, but for the most part I'll be here at Still Waters, except when I check on the farm. Nice to have hired help, you know."

"You worked hard on the farm."

"Now I hire people to labor for me." Dmitri smiled. "So you can consider me semi-retired since I'm not doing any work stateside with the exception of a part-time job at Still Salvage, if you have a position available."

As Briscoe watched the conversation between Dmitri and Mira, he suspected that Dmitri was only doing this to spend more time with his daughter. The multimillionaire did not need a part time job salvaging computer parts.

"All right. Send in your résumé, and someone will contact you when there's a job opening," Mira said.

"No fast track?"

"No favorites, Dad."

"How I love to hear you call me Dad." Dmitri's eyes watered.

Mira's phone buzzed.

"I have a meeting in fifteen minutes," Mira said. "Busy day."

"Y'all go ahead." Dmitri waved. "I'm going to stop by the clinic to check my blood pressure."

"Y'all? You're sounding more and more southern these days," Briscoe said.

"I'm trying to blend in." Dmitri grinned.

"Say hi to Ailey for us." Mira gave her dad a light hug.

"Will do." Dmitri quickened his steps toward the clinic.

"Briscoe, are you sure you're not mad at my dad?" Mira asked after Dmitri was gone.

"Not anymore. I passed the test, remember?"

"I'll always remember him as the former CIA agent who sent you to die in the desert of Libya."

"I survived."

"Then he implanted you with a tracker in the mountains of Bitteria so that the CIA could go in and find the missing SEAL team among Buchanan's cyborg army."

"Which they did."

"And now you're his daughter's boyfriend."

Briscoe prayed that he'd be her husband at some point. Soon, he hoped. He hadn't found the right diamond ring yet.

"Why are you so forgiving?" Mira asked.

"God first forgave me through Christ. Who am I to withhold forgiveness?"

"Your heart is right with God. I love you."

"I love you too." Briscoe swooped Mira off her feet and carried her across the grass in the direction of the Still Salvage barn.

"I can walk!" Mira put her arm around his neck so that she didn't fall off.

"I'm practicing."

"For what?"

"Carrying you over the threshold."

"The what?" Mira sounded surprised.

"You heard me."

"Are you serious?"

Briscoe couldn't stop smiling.

Dear Reader:

Thank you for reading *Zero Trust* (Binary Hackers Book 4). I hope you enjoyed this novel combining near-future technology and sweet Christian romance. If you like to read cyber and techno suspense thrillers without having to compromise your Christian faith, check out the rest of my Binary Hackers series, starting with *Zero Sum* (Binary Hackers Book 1), where we meet Mira and her father, Dmitri, for the first time. *Zero Sum* is the story of Leland's cousin, Cayson Yang, and his kill-switch cybernetic implant:

*Zero Sum* (Binary Hackers Book 1)
JanThompson.com/zerosum

You don't have to read the series in order, but it might make for more enjoyable "oh so that's why" moments if you do. For more details about these books and my other book collections, visit my author website at JanThompson.com, where you can also sign up for my book news mailing list.

Binary Hackers
JanThompson.com/binary
Jan's Mailing List:
JanThompson.com/newsletter

### Leland Yang-Joule is in various books!

Mira's hacker friend, Leland, has appeared as a secondary character in all of the Binary Hackers books as well as my other Christian romantic suspense books. We first meet her in *Once a Thief* (Protector Sweethearts Book 1), where private investigator Helen Hu asks for Leland's help to find her abducted mother in Europe. In the near future, Leland will have her own set of books dedicated to her work as an uber hacker. In the meantime, have you read these books in which Leland makes cameo appearances?

*Once a Thief* (Protector Sweethearts Book 1)
JanThompson.com/thief

*Never a Traitor* (Defender Sweethearts Book 1)

JanThompson.com/traitor

*Zero Sum* (Binary Hackers Book 1)
JanThompson.com/zerosum

### Esperanza Diaz-Mendenhall is also everywhere!

In *Zero Trust,* security expert Esperanza Diaz-Mendenhall is mentioned numerous times. She is an important supporting character in at least a few of my other novels. She will headline her own novel soon. In the meantime, look for Esperanza in:

*Reach for Me* (Vacation Sweethearts Book 2)
JanThompson.com/reach

*Wait for Me* (Vacation Sweethearts Book 3)
JanThompson.com/wait

*Once a Spy* (Protector Sweethearts Book 3)
JanThompson.com/spy

### Raynelle Glynn is in ONCE A SPY

*Once a Spy* is also where we first meet Raynelle under her maiden name, Raynelle Dryden. In *Once a Spy* (Protector Sweethearts Book 3), she has a love-hate relationship with billionaire treasure hunter Benjamin Glynn. Blackbeard's treasure map, Dogs of War drones, exoskeletons, and more all appear in this novel. We also meet Rulon Smith and Dakara Dermott. In many ways, *Once a Spy* is a springboard to my Binary Hackers series.

*Once a Spy* (Protector Sweethearts Book 3)
JanThompson.com/spy

Back to *Zero Trust*, if you have enjoyed this novel, would you please write a review? Reviews are helpful to readers who are new to my books. If you'd like to leave a review, follow this link to the online retailers carrying this book:

*Zero Trust* (Binary Hackers Book 4)
JanThompson.com/zerotrust

For now, *Zero Trust* is the last book in my Binary Hackers series. The next series that spins off of Binary Hackers will be Leland Yang-Joule's stories from the digital trenches. Until then, do visit my author website at JanThompson.com, where you can also sign up for my book news mailing list to be notified when the next books are released. My newsletters showcase book news and my life behind the scene.

Jan's Mailing List:
JanThompson.com/newsletter

If you haven't read the first book in the Binary Hackers series, turn the page for a sneak peek of *Zero Sum*.

**A broken hacker.**
**A brave FBI agent.**
**A deadly brain implant.**

In *Zero Sum* (Binary Hackers Book 1), FBI
Cybercrime Special Agent Stella Evans finds the

last surviving computer consultant who holds the key to destroying a terrorist organization's global network, but Cayson Yang may not live long enough to dismantle the computer system.

The Chaos...

Computer network specialist Cayson Yang's struggling network infrastructure company has received a rash of new clients lately, the total income of which finally puts Binary Systems, Inc., in the black for the first time ever. He is now able to give pay raises to himself and his business partner and cousin, Leland Yang-Joule, and bonuses to his employees. Cayson dreams of a bigger office space for them all.

Somewhere between two dollars in his bank account and a two-million-dollar computer network contract, Cayson finds himself in the crosshair of the world's most notorious terrorist organization that is now coming after him, his business partners, his family, and even relatives he doesn't know exist.

Ignoring repeated warning lights might have been Cayson's downfall, but it's too late for him to backtrack...

The Crime...

Assigned to the National Cyber Investigative Joint Task Force, FBI Special Agent Stella Evans finishes assisting her colleagues from the Counterterrorism Division to apprehend a notorious terrorist.

On trial in Europe for war crimes too numerous to list, Molyneux refuses to help the authorities dismantle her sophisticated international computer network. The only alternative is to find the architects of this network and hope they will cooperate.

Shutting down Molyneux's underground computer network is the best way to destroy those mercenary terrorists for hire. However, the terrorist organization doesn't want to be outdone. A successor is named, and they begin to kill off anyone who has worked on the underground network in the past.

The Crisis...

By the time Stella reaches the Binary Systems global headquarters in Atlanta, Georgia, most of the original computer specialists who worked for Molyneux are either dead or have disappeared—except their fearful leader, Cayson Yang, the final link, kept alive for reasons unknown.

Stella finds herself at a crossroad between duty and following Cayson and the cybernetic implants in his head. She stands to lose not only her carefully cultivated career but, more dangerously, her closely guarded heart as she decides what to do with the Pandora's box she has opened.

Zero Sum (Binary Hackers Book 1)
JanThompson.com/zerosum

Binary Hackers
JanThompson.com/binary

To receive book news from Jan Thompson:
JanThompson.com/newsletter

# ZERO SUM PROLOGUE
## SNEAK PEEK
### BINARY HACKERS BOOK 1

"This better pay off, Kel," Cayson Yang said when his employee and friend came back to their booth at a corner of the noisy convention center. "We paid five thousand dollars for this spot, and nobody has stopped by all morning. Day two."

All around their tiny booth were gargantuan displays from mega technology firms that Cayson's small computer consulting company could never hope to compete with. They were big, loud, noisy, and they had food. Which Kelvin Gallagher had been munching on as he made the rounds, leaving Cayson to manage the Yottaflops Data Storage LLC booth on his own.

Kelvin had a mouthful of snacks. He muttered

something about missing breakfast. It came out sounding like he was missing *butter*.

Or *buffer*, depending on if you were at work or home.

"There must be hundreds of tech expos in the southeast, and we had to pick this one where we're invisible," Cayson continued.

"We? You picked it," Kelvin reminded him.

"Well, I'm scolding myself right now." Cayson pointed to one of the booths nearby. It had a big poster of a bobblehead advertising 3D printing, and a long wraparound line of people. "We're in the wrong business."

Kelvin pulled something from his pocket. It was a bobblehead doll of himself.

"Whoa. So that's what they're doing over there?" Cayson asked.

"Yeah. You can ask them to print anything for you. The kid in front of me skipped away with a nerf gun that actually shoots darts. I got this." He shook his bobblehead.

"You do have a big head. How much did it cost you?"

Kelvin winked. "If you have to ask, you can't afford it."

Across another aisle, speakers blared loud

Bollywood music as a huge crowd gathered around a demonstration of graphics design innovations.

Cayson felt the urge to get off his folding chair and join the decibels of success.

Instead, he found himself tidying his empty counter, stacking up business cards and a sorry brochure he had printed off their office printer—because someone had forgotten to order new brochures.

*We're a digital company. We don't do paper. Save the trees!*

The IKEA countertop was slightly chipped on a couple of sides from when he and Kelvin had tried to offload it from the top of his hybrid vehicle on Monday morning. That was after the Atlanta police had given him a citation for dangerous driving.

How was he supposed to know that bungee cords had a breaking point?

His D in college physics hadn't helped.

"Maybe we need a bowl of candy," Kelvin suggested. "Food draws people."

"Candy is not food."

"A technicality." Kelvin downed a whole bottle of soda and smacked his lips. "Maybe it's the name of the company."

"What's wrong with Yottaflops?" Cayson had picked the name of the company carefully.

At this moment in his life, yotta was the largest metric unit.

Hence, *yottaflops*.

A bazillion floating point operations per second.

Ten to the power of twenty-four.

*That's some fast server.*

"The dichotomy in meanings is too obvious," Kelvin explained, as if he thought that his employer had missed the point. "If we're not talking server speed, but data storage, it should be YottaBytes."

"But we're not only doing data storage," Cayson countered. "We do primarily systems. Systems mean servers, and servers means FLOPS."

Kelvin pointed to the logo on his bright-yellow T-shirt. "This says *Data Storage*."

"Whatever you do, don't talk to Leland about this. She's been wanting to fold Yottaflops into our parent company, Binary Systems."

"One name to rule them all..."

"She has fifty-one percent of the company shares. If she says it costs too much money to run two separate companies, then that's the way it is." Cayson looked around, wondering where all the customers were. "It has already cost too much money to change everything. Bank cards, logos, door signs, checkbooks—"

"Whoa. What? Did you say checkbooks? Who uses checkbooks these days?"

"I do. And I had them specially printed. A lot of money has gone into this business and we're still not breaking even."

Cayson had sold his house to start Binary Systems, Inc. Then he created a branch to give Kelvin a job. It hadn't seemed ridiculous at first because Cayson felt great saving Kelvin.

Thing was, Cayson was not Kelvin's savior.

But the deed had been done.

Binary Systems had spawned off Yottaflops, and now Cayson owed the IRS money.

The companies had to succeed.

Cayson couldn't live in Mom's basement much longer. Pretty soon she would ask him to do more than just take out the trash. At least she had not yet suggested that he volunteer in her law office in exchange for free meals.

Well, she had been taking care of his cats when he was at work all day and night long.

"Whatever," Kelvin said. "It's your company. Say, when is Leland coming? I have to get back to the machine room. Our Dubai client wants his data backed up somewhere safe and offshore."

"Hush."

"Like anyone can hear us—or even cares." Kelvin put up a palm. "Sorry. I didn't mean that in a bad way. Obscurity has its benefits, you know, especially in our line of work."

Cayson said nothing.

"I'll stay if you want me to." Kelvin wadded up another candy wrapper and tossed it into the trash can under the counter.

"I don't think we'll have a lot of foot traffic the rest of the day. Why don't you go?"

"See you at the meeting." Kelvin shook his head. "Who in the world calls for a meeting at three in the morning?"

*Guilty as charged.*

Well, when the customer was paying half their income, Cayson had no choice but to comply, even if they wanted to talk business at a time convenient to them. It would not always be during the day in Cayson's time zone.

The perks and perils of having global clients.

Cayson watched Kelvin go. He meandered in and out of the booths, picking up snacks, brochures, and such.

Kelvin was a hard worker. Not as brilliant a hacker as Cayson's cousin and business partner, Leland, but he was a great system administrator. And he didn't need any sleep. He could fill in all night long and still function in the daytime.

Boisterous cheering across the aisle from the Bollywood booth made Cayson look that way.

He flinched.

Blocking his view was a ghost from his past, gliding into his booth.

Startled, Cayson gripped the counter and felt the chipped edge cut into his palm.

He couldn't remember her username. He had only seen her online. Never in person.

Didn't she live in Asia somewhere? Macau someplace?

What was she doing in the United States?

Something must be terribly wrong for her to show up here. Why here? Why now?

"Are you Cayson Yang?" She sounded like she was in a hurry.

Her accent was pretty good. She had said online that she had learned English by watching American television shows.

But that was eighteen months ago.

No one was supposed to contact anyone else on the team.

They had all agreed.

*What is she doing here?*

Cayson decided he had to have a talk with Dmitri about this breach of security.

"Who's asking for him?" Cayson replied.

"Do you always speak in third person?"

"Huh?"

"Your name tag says *Cayson Yang*."

"Oh." Cayson winced. *Note to self: stop wearing name tags.*

"How may I help you?" He started over, continuing his charade. *Definitely need to talk with Dmitri about this.*

"I have a warning for Ulysses."

*What warning?* "You mean a message?"

"A warning."

Only a small handful of people knew who Ulysses was.

And even fewer people knew where he had gone.

In fact, Cayson himself had no idea where Ulysses was at the moment. Only Ulysses's best friend knew, and the latter was incommunicado.

Cayson prayed to God for mercy. He had thought that blighted time in his career was long gone. How could it resurface now, when he was trying to make a legitimate, aboveboard living?

"He no longer works for me," he said. "He's off the grid."

Bollywood music thumped in his ears. People cheered and made a lot of noise.

Cayson saw the woman's lips move, but he couldn't hear anything.

She came around the counter.

Cayson felt a sudden splash of spit or liquid or something on his face.

His eyes reflexively shut, and his shoulders pulled back. He lost his balance, and fell backward, going down on the carpeted floor.

As he rolled, he felt a sharp, quick stab just above his left ear.

The pain shot through his skull.

He screamed.

# ZERO SUM CHAPTER 1
## SNEAK PEEK
### BINARY HACKERS BOOK 1

B y the time FBI Special Agent Stella Evans arrived in Atlanta and drove to the VenomLabs office complex in Marietta, the third victim had been dead for almost a day.

Stella's flight from DC had been full, and she'd had to change planes in Charlottesville because of engine trouble. If anything could be worse, Atlanta traffic might rate up there.

From the Hartsfield-Jackson Atlanta International Airport to Marietta, the drive had been a crawl through rush hour in the metropolis, with the late-afternoon traffic going in the same direction she was, where Interstates 75 and 85 merged.

Her stomach rumbled for dinner that wouldn't

come for another couple of hours. But she couldn't worry about that now.

Three deaths in a week.

Today, it had been another network specialist of Binary Systems, Inc.

This time he had not died by his own hands. Jamal Cruze had been found in a roadside ditch in Woodstock, Georgia, some ten feet away from his Ducati.

His head had exploded under his helmet.

Officers from the Woodstock Police Department and the Georgia Bureau of Investigation had been all over the place. Their reports would be shared with her, she had been told.

Stella had no jurisdiction over the dead body itself.

But she had jurisdiction over the implants in the victim's head.

If her hunch was correct, the implants would be the same as those found on the other two dead employees, whom Binary Systems had contracted to the National Security Agency, two days before Cayson Yang had disappeared.

If she was correct, then she could safely say that they had all originated from the same implant prototypes stolen from VenomLabs two years ago.

New and improved and deadly.

Meant for the NSA, not global terrorists.

Grigori Norton had been the first victim, hit on the night of the data storage convention as he watched an evening cooking show at his rental apartment in Fort Meade. His housekeeper had called 911. Police had arrived to the gruesome sight of a headless body.

Six hours and a continent away, in the Binary Systems office in Prague, Audrey Lindberg had gone outside the building for a smoke. When she didn't return to the process her team had been in the middle of, they sent someone to find her. And find her, he did—her head splattered like a smashed watermelon on the old cobblestone sidewalk.

That had been the pattern of death: exploding heads.

So. Grigori Norton. Audrey Lindberg. And now Jamal Cruze.

As for another two hackers—Vivek Rao and Danika Svoboda—they were presumed dead, although their bodies had never been found.

Stella feared that the next person could be Cayson Yang.

Dispatched by the National Cyber Investigative Joint Task Force to Atlanta because her partner, Jake Kessler, had decided to stay behind in Fort Meade, Stella's job this week was to hang out with the cybernetics division at VenomLabs and make sure the FBI wasn't left out of the loop.

Of course, it had helped her cause that she had worked with Cayson Yang before in Project Pericarp, in which Binary Systems had been paid ten million dollars to set up an underground network for a supposedly British company so that the NCIJT could track the cashflow of terrorism.

Sometime this morning, the Cobb County Medical Examiner's Office had delivered the extracted implants from poor Jamal Cruze to VenomLabs. The implants had been badly damaged, but they were something to look at.

*I suppose.*

VenomLabs was the only contractor with the Defense Advanced Research Projects Agency. Whatever VenomLabs said, everyone believed.

Who watched VenomLabs, really?

VenomLabs owned a laboratory complex near the Dobbins Air Reserve Base in Marietta, just outside the Interstate 285 loop.

By the time Stella reached the front gate of the unmarked building, it was almost six o'clock. After this evening's meeting, she'd check into her hotel, get some sleep, and then drive to Chamblee the next morning, bright and early, for a NCIJTF meeting at the FBI field office.

For some reason, they didn't want to meet on-site at VenomLabs.

Something was off, but Stella couldn't put her finger on—

Her iPhone buzzed.

Jake Kessler.

The special agent in charge of her.

They had both been assigned to the NCIJTF, but Stella wouldn't do a thing unless Kessler gave her the all clear.

Stella sat in her parked car. She glanced around to make sure the windows had been rolled up. "Yes, sir?"

Excited about the NCIJTF collaboration with CIA field agents in Europe, Kessler was talking a mile a minute. All Stella could do was listen.

They had found Cayson Yang, and he was alive.

That was all Stella needed to know. "You want me to fly out to Istanbul?"

"Yeah. We have people keeping an eye on him, but they don't want to spook him," Kessler said. "A familiar face might help."

"What's he doing over there?"

"He seems to be checking items off his bucket list."

*Yikes.* "So that's why he's in Istanbul? Taking pictures?"

"He knows what we're up against. And we might be running out of time."

Stella had known Cayson for some years now. They had brushed shoulders again in recent months after the FBI had found out about the sale of MedusaNet to Molyneux's organization and had begun tracking their activities across the network.

Even with Molyneux on trial for international war crimes, there had not been any lull. Someone else had taken over the organization and was supposedly planning attacks on American soil.

*Who is Molyneux's successor?*

"If I fly out tonight, I'll be there tomorrow afternoon," Stella said. "Will I be too late?"

"Atlanta to Istanbul would take anywhere from twelve to sixteen hours or more, depending on how many stops you make."

Stella waited. She knew that Kessler would have a solution, or at least suggest options. He had been pretty determined to get Molyneux and had succeeded spectacularly—and in his own words, unexpectedly.

"I might have a faster way," Kessler said. "Pack your bags."

"My bags haven't been unpacked. I just arrived."

"Right. Wait for my text. I'll see if you can get a ride from Dobbins to Istanbul."

Dobbins Air Reserve Base was a couple of exits away from VenomLabs. Going against traffic, she could be there anytime Kessler wanted her to be.

"Who's going to babysit VenomLabs?"

"I'll take care of that. You and I will meet in Istanbul and go from there. And, Evans?"

"Yes, sir?"

"Trust no one. Not even me."

It was the strangest instruction Stella had ever heard.

# ACKNOWLEDGMENTS

Many thanks to my Georgia Press publishing team for keeping up with my writing schedule.

Three outstanding editors read my novel. Thank you to editors Dori Harrell and Lesley McDaniel for copyediting and proofreading *Zero Trust*. Thank you to Kim Kemery for proofreading the final file. You all rock!

Thank you to my Advanced Reader Copy (ARC) team, who love reading new books. What takes me months and years to write, they devour in a matter of hours. I'm happy that they love the books I create in my story world. More to come, readers!

For winter camping tips, I thank my husband, who has hiked and camped more frequently in the old days than I had. Thanks for confirming everything I thought to be true about camping in the great outdoors of Georgia. One nice thing about camping in the colder months is that there are no bugs, especially the notorious mosquitoes.

I am grateful to God for my husband and son for their support and encouragement. I also thank God for my parents and my three brothers for my happy and memorable childhood. I'll always remember my beloved mother and my late father for having instilled in me the love of reading and writing from a very early age. I miss my father here on earth, but I will see him again in heaven someday.

Most of all, I am eternally thankful to my Lord and Savior, Jesus Christ, who died on the cross to save me from my sins and rose again from the grave to give me eternal life. Without Him, I can write nothing (John 15:5).

Jan Thompson
John 3:16

# BOOKS BY JAN THOMPSON

## CHRISTIAN ROMANTIC SUSPENSE & BEACH ROMANCE

BINARY HACKERS (Near-Future Inspirational Romantic Thrillers)

- Book 1: Zero Sum
- Book 2: Zero Day
- Book 3: Zero Base
- Book 4: Zero Trust

PROTECTOR SWEETHEARTS (Christian Romantic Suspense)

- Book 1: Once a Thief
- Book 2: Once a Hero

- Book 3: Once a Spy
- Book 4: Twice a Fighter
- Book 5: Twice a Convict
- Book 6: Twice a Soldier

## DEFENDER SWEETHEARTS (Christian Romantic Suspense)

- Book 1: Never a Traitor
- Book 2: Never a Hostage
- Book 3: Never a Fugitive
- Book 4: Always a Maverick
- Book 5: Always a Champion
- Book 6: Always a Guardian

## SAVANNAH SWEETHEARTS (Christian Coastal City & Beach Town Romance)

- Book 1: Ask You Later
- Book 2: Know You More
- Book 3: Tell You Soon (Romance with Suspense)
- Book 4: Draw You Near
- Book 5: Cherish You So
- Book 6: Walk You There

- Book 7: Love You Always (Romance with Suspense)
- Book 8: Kiss You Now
- Book 9: Find You Again
- Book 10: Wish You Joy (Christmas Year Round)
- Book 11: Call You Home
- Book 12: Let You Go

VACATION SWEETHEARTS (Christian Travel Romance)

- Book 1: Smile for Me
- Book 2: Reach for Me (Romance with Suspense)
- Book 3: Wait for Me (Romance with Suspense)
- Book 4: Look for Me (Romance with Suspense)
- Book 5: Pray for Me
- Book 6: Care for Me
- Book 7: Cheer for Me

SEASIDE CHAPEL (Christian Small Town Beach Romance)

- Book 1: His Longing Heart (second edition of *Share with Me*)
- Book 2: His Wake-Up Call (second edition of *Step with Me*)
- Book 3: His Morning Kiss (previously published as *Sing with Me*)
- Book 4: His Quiet Serenade
- Book 5: His Waiting Love
- Book 6: His Beach Retreat

Subscribe to Jan Thompson's mailing list:
JanThompson.com/newsletter

# BINARY HACKERS

Like more suspense with your Christian romance? Like to read suspense thrillers? If you're looking for clean near-future romantic suspense without compromising the Christian faith, these books are for you.

From *USA Today* bestselling author Jan Thompson come these inspirational near-future cyberthrillers combining technothriller and romance, starting with Binary Hackers that feature computer specialists living at the edge of cyberspace, where they have to juggle being law-abiding truth-telling Christians while carrying out their assignments by any and all means possible.

The Binary Hackers series is set in the same story world as Jan's other books, and characters from the other series may make cameo appearances in this series and vice versa.

JanThompson.com/binary

- Book 1: Zero Sum
- Book 2: Zero Day
- Book 3: Zero Base
- Book 4: Zero Trust

# PROTECTOR SWEETHEARTS

Private investigator Helen Hu and her associates specialize in searching for missing persons and hunting for lost treasures. Join them in their adventure suspense around the world in *USA Today* bestselling author Jan Thompson's Protector Sweethearts, a series of Christian Romantic Suspense with a side of mystery. Protector Sweethearts is a spin-off of Savannah Sweethearts and Vacation Sweethearts.

JanThompson.com/protector

- Book 1: Once a Thief

- Book 2: Once a Hero
- Book 3: Once a Spy
- Book 4: Twice a Fighter
- Book 5: Twice a Convict
- Book 6: Twice a Soldier

## DEFENDER SWEETHEARTS

Defender Sweethearts is a sister series to the Protector Sweethearts Christian romantic suspense collection. While the heroes in Protector Sweethearts search for lost treasures and lost people, the Defender Sweethearts novels focus on protecting the helpless and hopeless. The main characters in Defender Sweethearts come from the supporting cast in Protector Sweethearts.

JanThompson.com/defender

- Book 1: Never a Traitor

- Book 2: Never a Hostage
- Book 3: Never a Fugitive
- Book 4: Always a Maverick
- Book 5: Always a Champion
- Book 6: Always a Guardian

# SAVANNAH SWEETHEARTS

Welcome to the new south! From *USA Today* bestselling author Jan Thompson come these clean and wholesome, sweet and inspirational Christian romances set on the romantic beaches of Tybee Island and in the coastal town of Savannah, Georgia.

Meet a group of multiracial and multiethnic churchgoing Christians who love the Lord, work hard in their careers, and seek God's will for their love lives. Against a backdrop of ocean, sand, and sun, these inspirational romances showcase aspects of the human need for God and for one another. Have some tea, settle in a comfortable reading chair, and enjoy these sweet celebrations of faith, hope, and love in Jesus Christ.

JanThompson.com/savannah

- Book 1: Ask You Later (Artist Romance)
- Book 2: Know You More (Multiracial Romance)
- Book 3: Tell You Soon (Romance with Suspense)
- Book 4: Draw You Near (International Romance)
- Book 5: Cherish You So (Wheelchair BillionaireRomance)
- Book 6: Walk You There (Tour Guide Romance)
- Book 7: Love You Always (Romance with Suspense)
- Book 8: Kiss You Now (Multiracial Romance)
- Book 9: Find You Again (Multiracial Romance)
- Book 10: Wish You Joy (Christmas-Themed Romance)
- Book 11: Call You Home (Deaf Chef Romance)

- Book 12: Let You Go (Romance with Suspense)

# VACATION SWEETHEARTS

Travel with our friends from Savannah, Georgia, to the coast and to the mountains. Cheer them on as they celebrate the immeasurable grace and undeserved mercy of God through Jesus Christ.

The Vacation Sweethearts novels are a spin-off of Jan's Savannah Sweethearts series, and fans will recognize familiar faces from Riverside Chapel, a church in the coastal city of Savannah, Georgia. In fact, we might even visit the beach town of Tybee Island from time to time to visit old friends and beloved families...

JanThompson.com/vacation

- Book 0 (Prequel): Time for Me
- Book 1: Smile for Me (International Romance)
- Book 2: Reach for Me (Romance with Suspense)
- Book 3: Wait for Me (Romance with Suspense)
- Book 4: Look for Me (Romance with Suspense)
- Book 5: Pray for Me (International Romance)
- Book 6: Care for Me
- Book 7: Cheer for Me (International Romance)

# SEASIDE CHAPEL

Welcome to *USA Today* bestselling author Jan Thompson's Seaside Chapel Christian beach romance series. These novels are set on real-life St. Simon's Island, Georgia—a beach town where history is all around and the future is a moment away—and the neighboring fictitious Seaside Island, where the rich and famous live.

Savor the small-town atmosphere and the warm southern beaches of St. Simon's Island and the idyllic Golden Isles along the Atlantic Ocean. Enjoy the music of the orchestra and hymns of the church, and hang out with our Christian friends who attend Seaside Chapel, a little church by the sea known for its beach weddings and fair share of love and life.

As these Christians grow in their knowledge and understanding of God, they are tested in their spiritual maturity, their love lives, and their relationships with others. Share their heartaches and healing, and cheer them on as they celebrate faith, family, and friends.

JanThompson.com/seaside

- Book 1: His Longing Heart (second edition of Share with Me)
- Book 2: His Wake-Up Call (second edition of Step with Me)
- Book 3: His Morning Kiss (previously published as Sing with Me)
- Book 4: His Quiet Serenade
- Book 5: His Waiting Love
- Book 6: His Beach Retreat

# ABOUT JAN THOMPSON

*USA Today* bestselling author Jan Thompson writes clean and wholesome contemporary Christian romance with elements of women's fiction, Christian romantic suspense with an air of mystery, and inspirational international thrillers with threads of sweet Christian romance. Jan's books are for readers who love inspiring stories of faith, hope, and love in Jesus Christ.

Raised on a tropical island in the eastern hemisphere, Jan now lives and writes in the western hemisphere. Her international background gives her a unique multicultural and multiracial perspective to her novels and books. The island has never left her, and she reminisces about beach life in her beach romance novels.

When Jan is not busy writing small-town stories, she writes big-city romantic suspense and international technothrillers, a nod to her previous career in computer science. She weaves technology with human interests, reflecting the current and future digital world. And romance. There's always romance.

Beyond the printed page, Jan is a wife, mother, family scribe, avid reader, occasional artist, erstwhile pianist, and chief of staff to the family cat.

Find out more about Jan Thompson:
JanThompson.com

Subscribe to Jan's book news mailing list:
JanThompson.com/newsletter

*For God so loved the world*
*that He gave His only begotten Son,*
*that whoever believes in Him*
*should not perish*
*but have everlasting life.*
—John 3:16